Dickinson, Peter,
1927-

eleton-in-waiting

$16.45

DATE		

SKELETON-IN-WAITING

SKELETON-IN-WAITING

Peter Dickinson

PANTHEON BOOKS NEW YORK

All rights reserved under International and Pan-American Copyright
Conventions. Published in the United States by Pantheon Books, a division of
Random House, Inc., New York. Originally published in Great Britain by the
Bodley Head Ltd., London, in 1989.

Library of Congress Cataloging-in-Publication Data

Dickinson, Peter, 1927–
    Skeleton-in-waiting / by Peter Dickinson.
        p.   cm.
    ISBN 0-394-58002-8
    I. Title.
    PR6054.I35S57   1989
    823'.914—dc19   89-42561

Display Typography by Tara Devereux
Manufactured in the United States of America

First American Edition

NOTE

We are all, of course, the prisoners of our pasts. This can apply even to imaginary people with imaginary pasts. Some of the central characters of this book are the prisoners of a past set out in *King and Joker*, in which it is assumed that Edward, Duke of Clarence, elder brother of the Duke of York who later in the real world became King George V, did not die in 1887 but lived to inherit as King Victor I, being then succeeded by his grandson, the present King Victor II. The resulting family tree is set out overleaf. The only point that might be added is that the king is in fact bigamously married to Queen Isabella (Bella) and her secretary Ms Anona Fellowes (Nonny), and that Princess Louise is really Nonny's daughter. Since *King and Joker* has of course not been published in its own imaginary world, this relationship is a very well-kept secret.

FAMILY TREE

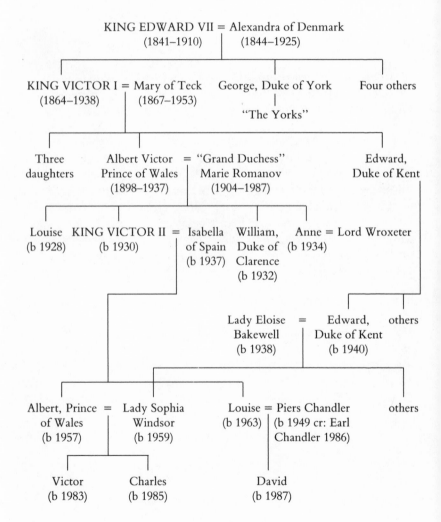

KING EDWARD VII = Alexandra of Denmark
(1841–1910)   (1844–1925)

KING VICTOR I = Mary of Teck   George, Duke of York   Four others
(1864–1938)   (1867–1953) |
                                        "The Yorks"

Three   Albert Victor = "Grand Duchess"   Edward,
daughters   Prince of Wales   Marie Romanov   Duke of Kent
               (1898–1937)   (1904–1987)

Louise   KING VICTOR II = Isabella   William,   Anne = Lord Wroxeter
(b 1928)   (b 1930)   of Spain   Duke of   (b 1934)
                            (b 1937)   Clarence
                                        (b 1932)

                              Lady Eloise = Edward,   others
                              Bakewell   Duke of Kent
                              (b 1938)   (b 1940)

Albert, Prince = Lady Sophia   Louise = Piers Chandler   others
of Wales   Windsor   (b 1963) | (b 1949 cr: Earl
(b 1957)   (b 1959) | Chandler 1986)

     Victor   Charles   David
     (b 1983)   (b 1985)   (b 1987)

OCTOBER 1987

I

"*Is that you?*"

"*. . .*"

"*Right. Now, listen. I've been thinking about what you said and I've worked out who it was you were talking about. In my book that wasn't politics. It was plain murder.*"

"*. . .*"

"*I know that's what you think. All I can tell you is if it had been anyone else than you I'd've gone straight to the police.*"

"*. . .?*"

"*Soon as I've finished talking to you. Give you a chance to get out.*"

"*. . .*"

"*You mean they'd kill you, just for talking to me without their say-so?*"

"*. . .*"

"*Oh, God! How stupid can you get! Why'd you ever want to get yourself into this? And me too, now? What are we going to do?*"

"*. . .*"

"*Oh, God, I suppose so. If you'll promise me nothing's going to happen before then. But I'm telling you this — if you don't come up with some kind of out for both of us, something which means nobody getting hurt or killed, I'm going to the police, no matter.*"

"*. . .*"

"*You do that.*"

I

"Tell me, ma'am, what does it feel like to wake with the knowledge that on average some twenty thousand of your fellow countrymen have been sleeping with you in their dreams?"

"I never give it a thought. It's just one of those things."

The don, a colleague of Piers, had been half drunk, or he wouldn't have asked, but Louise hadn't minded; her answer had been almost true. She must have been about sixteen when the bit of research on the erotic fantasies of the male Briton in relation to the royal family had first been published, and it had bothered her a bit back then, but in recent years never, not till this morning. Why now should she wake from the nightmare image of that immense and silent queue stretching from the bedroom door, down the stairs, along the hall, out past the bored security guards, along the lime avenue, through the gates, but then not into the Bedfordshire countryside which in real life lay around Quercy, but into a dream landscape composed of all her favourite childhood places, Windsor Home Park with its ponds, the Dee at Balmoral with Father impatiently fishing, a Spanish beach with Mother embroidering beneath a purple umbrella?

Louise stretched out a hand to feel for Piers. The discovery that he wasn't there prolonged the nightmare a second or two until she was properly awake and knew the reason — today there was the Visiting Head and they'd both be on parade, so Piers would have slipped away at five to get a stint of work in, deep in his own imaginary maze while she'd been constructing her horrible dream. She reached out an arm and turned up the volume of the intercom till she could hear the come-and-go of Davy's breath. Steady as a soldier. Right through from the two o'clock feed again. Terrific. She left the volume up and switched on the radio.

". . . and finally Jersey. South-east by east; haze, four miles; a thousand and thirteen, falling slowly. And that is the end of the shipping forecast and reports from coastal stations."

Pause. The pips. Six o'clock on the morning of Friday the thirtieth of October. News briefing.

"The death has been announced from Kensington Palace of . . ."

Louise had half-known before the sentence began. There had been that particular tone in the announcer's voice while he was reading the time and date — something Family, and serious. Given a few more seconds she might have gauged exactly how serious, and from that deduced, though she had heard nothing about Granny being ill, that it could only be her.

". . . of Princess Marie, Dowager Princess of Wales, mother of His Majesty King Victor, following a domestic accident. No details have yet been announced, but it is understood that the accident took place late yesterday evening. The Princess was immediately taken to St Mary's Hospital, Paddington, but was found to be dead on arrival. King Victor and Queen Isabella arrived soon after. A statement is expected to be issued from Buckingham Palace within the next hour.

"Now the rest of the news. The pressure upon the dollar has . . ."

Louise stopped listening and lay with closed eyes, staring into the past. Granny, last of the Romanovs. (Not true, of course — there were dozens of perfectly authentic Romanovs around the world, growing vines in Tuscany, dealing in real estate in California, racing horses in France, playboying in the West Indies, but Granny always tried to make out that their blood ran less purely Romanov than hers.) Talons across the harp-strings, glittering green eyes, carroty hair, sickly wafts of *Chypre*. A domestic accident. How she would have despised the adjective.

The telephone rang. Too soon for the switchboard to be open. Only Family knew the other number.

"Father? I'm sorry."

"You've heard?"

"On the news just now. What happened?"

"Far as anyone can make out she fell off one of the pianos trying to catch that parrot of hers. I thought I'd ring you first, seeing you were about the only one who could stand her. Broke her neck. Death pretty well instantaneous."

"That's something. I suppose it'll be court mourning."

"Yes, of course — don't know how long. There aren't any decent precedents. Whatsername, George Three's mama, must have been the last."

"It would have been months back then."

"Three or four weeks should do it. Anyway, it lets you off this do today."

"Great. Granny would have wanted months, too. I say, why don't you have a memorial concert to make up?"

"Possible."

"Get a lot of famous musicians who loathe each other onto the same platform. She'd really appreciate that."

"Bella wouldn't let us lark around that much. Anyway the funeral comes first."

"Not a Russian one, please. Kissing her live was bad enough."

"Don't be disgusting. It looks like Thursday week, give the foreign lot a chance to show up. You don't sound too upset."

"I don't know. I suppose I'll miss her — like a comic on the telly, or a smelly old dog you've got used to. Piers will be pleased about the mourning."

"Tell him we'll claw it back. But listen, Lulu, while I've got you, there's something else. I'm afraid you're not going to like this . . . Hang on . . . yes . . . OK . . . I'll have to call you back, Lulu. Ten minutes?"

"Provided Davy stays asleep."

"OK."

She hung up. Not going to like what? Some fuss with the hacks? Trouble with Aunt Eloise Kent? Might be anything. Mother was going to need a bit of help with Aunt Bea, though. Granny had exploited and tormented Aunt Bea mercilessly, treating her more as butt and drudge than the companion-cum-lady-in-waiting she was supposed to be, but still Aunt Bea was the only person who would be genuinely grieved by Granny's death. Apart from that? A lot of it was automatic. The whole machinery of a royal funeral would trundle gloomily gleaming from storage to perform for the first time in . . . how long? Ages. Aunt Rosie had died when Louise had been about seven, but she hadn't been given the full works. The last real turn-out must have been for

4

Great-grandmama, Queen Mary, back in 1953. Over thirty years. Not that Granny would get anything as fancy as that. The Palace would brief the hacks that it was because she'd never been Queen, but everyone would know it was really because she'd been a joke, or a pest, or both together.

No point either in thinking much about your own rearrangements. First you had to have the Guidance. By now Nonny and Sir Sam and Commander Tank and a few others would be sitting over the diaries with the Amstrad sorting it all out. P. of W. at airport to greet Visiting Head. Black armbands for Guard of Honour. Retain State Drive in coaches, but without H. and H.M. All flags at half mast on route. Contact FCO re bigwig to accompany Head to Opera tonight, ditto Jockey Club re races tomorrow. (Lucky deceased equivalent of Mother of Chief — important figure in Head's culture.) Banquet tomorrow night? Stick to that, because HM down to make speech mollifying hurt feelings over ITV programme exposing uses of torture in Head's prisons. Sunday, thank God, he wants to himself, Palace having declined request to supply dancing-boys. P. and P. of W. to see bastard off at airport on Monday. No public events for His M Monday, Her M to open new ward at Great Ormond Street — she'll insist on sticking to that but cancel kids releasing balloons at entrance . . . and so on, gradually diminishing grief for the royal loss being measured down by calibrations invisible to anyone not wearing Palace spectacles — if Mother's jaunt to the hospital had been scheduled for a week later, then it might have been deemed proper for her to watch the balloons soaring towards the rain-clouds.

It would be a good hour before they retrieved Louise's engagements on the Amstrad and went through them and then rang Joan with the Guidance. Of course, if there was anything HRH felt strongly about they'd be happy to reconsider . . . Meanwhile, all Louise had to wonder about was what she could do with her day off. Her main impulse was to call Piers on the house phone and tell him about the Visiting Head being off so why didn't he come back to bed and finish his stint at a sensible time of day? No good. He'd been at it for an hour by now, and his mind would still be deep in the maze. Who wants to cuddle with a zombie? On the other hand, once he was through with it he'd take the rest of the day off without a murmur — three hours of Artificial Intelligence and he was mentally exhausted, which meant as far as Louise was concerned that he became normal, the man she had almost instantaneously fallen in love with, fought to marry, and still adored with a vehemence that alarmed and even distressed a whole section of her conscious self, the part whose training had been based on the unspoken premise that the one thing a princess cannot afford is emotion too strong to control. But, out of unpredictable ambush, this inner tiger had sprung.

The actual location of the ambush had been the university of which Louise was Chancellor. Her Vice-Chancellor, still at seventy-five as pushy as any politician, had decided that there might be publicity to be gained if after one degree-giving ceremony HRH were to meet informally with some of the younger fellows. The cut-off line for youth had been thirty-seven, so Piers had just counted and had come, reluctantly, in his only suit, straight from an AI session in which he had made what he had then believed to be a breakthrough, though it had turned out to be only another of the phantoms that beckoned through his maze. To accentuate the theme of youth the Vice-Chancellor had had a student jazz group playing in one of the rooms, and during small talk Piers and Louise had discovered their shared lack of enthralment with all forms of music. Tin ear had called to tin ear, and in Piers's case the call had been expressed in terms of surreal distaste, so that Louise had broken the decorum of Chancellorship by laughing aloud. The bleating of the goat excites the tiger.

Sometimes she wondered whether it had been love at all, at first, or merely a rebellion by the rest of her against the willed, trained self which she had thought of since childhood as the princessing machine. Father was extremely broad-minded, as monarchs go, Mother by instinct less so, though with a fathomless capacity to sympathise, but both had considered Piers wholly unsuitable as royal spouse and incredible as a member of the Family. So had Piers himself. When he had at last acknowledged his own tiger (more indolent and amenable than Louise's, she was aware) he had set out his terms in a document which had brought on one of Father's

6

coruscations of fury — an absolute classic, according to Nonny, just like the old days — detailing how much of the royal life he was prepared to live and how much not. Of course, he had stuck to his bargain, accepting the unwanted earldom, smiling and nodding to High Sheriffesses who embarked on intelligent questions about his work, judging rhubarb jam made by classes of eight-year-olds, applauding the traditional music of the Upper Gambo (nose-flute, two-stringed twanger and oil-drum flogged with bike-chain) and so on, but that didn't make him any more suitable or credible. Perhaps, Louise thought, that was all she had fallen in love with. Perhaps, in fact, it hadn't been love at all, but a sort of frenzy to be herself, to demonstrate by the enormous publicity of a royal wedding (the hacks and politicians had had an absolute field day) that she could make her own choices in spite of everything, and that the princessing machine, though it might be the public's servant, wasn't her mistress. Was that really all? No, but it had been part of it, an ingredient, a spice in the passion. It was why she was always going to love him more than he loved her. It didn't matter.

A flutter from the baby-alarm, not a whimper but a movement. Louise was out from under the duvet and half-way into her dressing-gown when the telephone rang again.

"Something I wasn't going to like," she said.

"Afraid so. You remember those buggers who had a go at Mother and me in Chester?"

Louise seemed to feel her body go rubbery-cold before her mind had taken the question in. It was the word "Chester" that triggered that response. The bomb had gone off prematurely, killing the dog who had found it and his handler, as well as the woman who had been putting the cushions out. They'd been the only ones close. The other injuries hadn't been serious, because it had been only a small bomb, in one of the cushions. It would gave gone off when Father sat on it. The dais had been checked already, several times. If the woman had been less attractive, and if the dog-handler hadn't wanted an excuse to chat her up . . .

"I thought they were all in gaol," she said.

"That lot, yes. They were a crack-pot little group and we think we got all the active ones. The Garda has been keeping

7

an eye on the known sympathisers. Now they've told us Gorman's brother has disappeared."

"What does that mean?"

"Can't tell. The brother was said to have been against Chester, but they're one of those Celtic families. Fairly unreadable to outsiders. Our people have a hunch he might try something to get Gorman out. That's all we've got."

"I suppose it means tighter bloody security."

"For a week or two, anyway. Will you talk to Piers?"

"Piers?"

"If they want to get Gorman out the obvious thing is a hostage. He might look a softer target than some of us."

"But we'd never . . . I mean, whoever they took . . . Can't they see . . . ?

"People in their position don't think in those terms. You're frustrated of what you regard as your legitimate desires, and your instinct is to take violent action. You rationalise your instinct by persuading yourself that the violence will have the effect you desire. For that to be the case, the nature of the real world has to be adjusted to allow such a chain of cause and effect to remain valid. There's all sorts of other reasons why Gorman's brother should have disappeared, if he has. And if that *is* the reason, there are other courses of action he may have in mind, and other targets at least as likely — ambassadors and so on. Just because it was us at Chester it doesn't have to be us again, only our security people are forced to act on the assumption of a risk to us. OK?"

"I'll do my best with Piers. That all?"

"Think so. Good girl. Look after yourself."

Louise put the telephone down and turned towards the nursery door. The triggered response to the word "Chester" had left her. This was just another security scare, the sort of nuisance that happened half a dozen times a year one way or another. You got used to it. She had heard no more sounds on the alarm but since she was up, and Davy would be waking any minute now . . .

Janine was by the cot, but had heard the movement of the door, and turned.

"Hey," whispered Louise. "This is my night on. You're supposed to be still asleep."

8

Janine widened her eyes, earnest as a child. She was plump-petite, like a Russian doll from near the smaller end of the set. Her pink quilted dressing-gown and yellow pyjamas added to the look of vulnerable innocence. "Sorry, ma'am," she whispered. "I forgot. Just woke, and thought I'd heard him thinking of crying."

"It must have been a bird. I had the alarm right up. You go back to bed — but listen, I've got the day off all of a sudden, so I'll cope till, oh, let's say half past nine. OK?"

"If you're sure, ma'am . . ."

"Yes, of course. Sleep well."

"Thank you, ma'am."

Louise watched her go with satifaction. Janine was just right, chosen for what everyone else had said were the wrong reasons — younger than Louise herself, straight from her training, so that Davy was her first baby, and — this mattered as much as anything — small. She fitted exactly with Louise's idea of what a nursery should be.

After nearly a year it still took Louise an effort of will to think of Quercy as home. Sometimes she imagined herself an alternative life. Suppose, for instance, we'd had a revolution like the one in Russia, of course there'd have been no question of Great-grandpapa and Great-grandmama and the great-aunts and great-uncles being shot in a cellar like the poor Romanovs — no, they'd just have been demoted to the ranks. Father would have been an ordinary doctor. Louise would have gone to the university as an ordinary student and met Piers somehow (all roads had to meet at that crossways, however you juggled history) and fallen in love and they'd have married or perhaps just decided to live together and started off in some ramshackle flat, she biking to her ordinary job and getting back in the evening festooned with carrier-bags . . . that might have felt like home, a nest she'd made, a lair she had to sweep and tidy for herself. But Quercy . . . it wasn't the house's fault. Or anyone's. It had to be big, for a start, with room for office staff and servants and drivers and a flat for Joan and Derek, and a suite for the odd lady-in-waiting, all that. No way it wasn't going to look a bit pompous. Then there was security. Security had turned down two other possible houses because they weren't happy with the perimeters; either of them might have done in the old days, though there'd always been snoopers, professional and amateur, and regicidal loonies, besides the extraordinary number of lonely and inadequate citizens who believed that all their problems would be solved if only they could get to chat in private with this or that member of the Family — like a psychic version of the Royal Touch. But now there were potential regicides who weren't loonies. Ten years ago Louise used often to walk, with one detective a few paces behind her but otherwise alone, from Kensington Palace across to Holland Park Comprehensive, and back again after school. Unthinkable since Chester. You lived in a sort of invisible force-field which moved when you moved, arriving with sniffer-dogs anywhere you were planned to visit a couple of days before you came and then surrounding you all the time you were there, armed and watchful on rooftops while you shook hands and fielded posies and chatted and moved on. Quercy was late Georgian, civilised, bland, symbolic of an era of peace, but for all that Davy, like his ancestors in the bloody centuries before, had been born in a fortress.

It had been a two-and-a-half-million-pound present from the father of the bride.

"I suppose it'll do," the bride had said.

"Good as anywhere else," the groom had answered.

Piers's only demands had been that they should live within driving distance of the university and that there should be one room where he could get a good fug up. He felt no need for a place he could think of as home. His home was himself, his habits and a very few possessions, like the blue mug he used at breakfast and the long-case clock he wound on Tuesdays. He created his notion of home as he had created himself, out of almost nothing. Even his name was one he had chosen when he was sixteen. No past contributed, no parents, no photographs of childhood, no mementoes. He had been dis-covered as a week-old baby on the back seat of a bus in a depot in Coventry. Later, of course, there were memories, but only if you asked, and then just lifeless dates and places — orphanage, schools, scholarships. No friends from before university. No one and nowhere he felt any wish to see again.

Louise by contrast had so much past that sometimes she felt

she existed in the present only as a dimensionless moving point, there to create fresh pasts by the ripple of its track. For a start there was the past stored in the public memory — hardly a week could have gone by since she was born without her picture appearing somewhere in newspapers or on TV. Last month a souvenir christening mug, five shillings new in 1963, had been sold at Bonhams for two hundred quid (Albert's fetched only fifty because he was heir to the throne, so they were commoner). And the past beyond that — one person in three in the street, if you'd asked them, could probably have named her paternal ancestors back through five generations, which they couldn't have done for themselves. Then inside that immense public past there was the semi-public Family past, the comings and goings of ramified relatives, Yorks, Kents, Spanish and Russian and Greek royals, Mountbattens and so on, a banyan of family trees, parts of the grove open for everyone to see, other bits in deep shadow, secret, merely guessed at by outsiders. And then inward to the past of the personal Family, Father, Mother, Nonny, Albert, and then Louise's own private and treasured past, the central memories which had grown with her, made her, become her. Above all the network of places — the Palace, Balmoral, Windsor, Sandringham — which she collectively regarded as home.

Moving into Quercy Louise had found herself at a loss, even in the most superficial matters such as choosing a wallpaper for the dining-room. The rooms of a proper home had existing wallpaper, which belonged; when you decided to change it you did so from a known base, a feel for the function of that room in your own psychic architecture. What did you do, confronted with a blank like Quercy? Louise's answer had been to get a cousin of Nonny's who did that sort of thing professionally, to make the decisions. For form's sake there'd be a pretence of consultation and she'd rejected two or three ideas saying she didn't like that colour, but with one exception she had let Quercy happen, and then found that she tended to feel as though she and Piers were the only guests in a comfortable but dull country hotel.

The exception was the nursery. Louise knew what a nursery should look like and feel like. She couldn't have everything — the fire was no good for crumpets and it was all a bit new, without the haunting sense of the procession of children who had passed through it, mottling and abrading, trying whether this chair would break or that chest push over, producing spillage and spewage, testing crayons on bare bits of wall, mountaineering along shelving and fighting toy wars behind battlements of books. But most of it was pretty well right. There were the rocking-horse and the pouffe and the Margaret Tarrant print of All Creatures Great and Small and the cardboard parrot and the Mickey Mouse clock (though it ran off a battery and kept perfect time) and the toy-chest with buttoned corduroy cover and the tall chair with tray and counting-frame and the smell of ironed linen and damp rusks and talcum. And, more important than anything, the right-shaped nanny. Small and neat, but cuddly. Watching Janine make her way back to bed Louise envisaged not the past but the future, a vista of children, and grandchildren, and great-grandchildren even, in whose own lives and memories that Russian-doll figure would become a much-loved landmark.

She gave the dim-switch a half turn and stole to the cot. Davy was lying on his front with his head turned sideways and his right arm crooked up on the mattress in a *Great Dictator* salute. His breathing faltered in its rhythm, then steadied as he relapsed into that almost-too-perfect look which small children somehow put on in sleep. He'd be awake in a few minutes, so Louise stayed where she was, looking down. She had been leaning over the cot for a good half-minute before she realised that something was missing. Normally, if she stood like this, at this time of day, waiting over the cot for her son to wake, she experienced a faint but definite surge of maternal emotion, too primitive and physical to count as love, seeming to emerge from the pit of her stomach and flood through her body like a drug injected into the bloodstream. Not today. Perhaps she was too wide awake, after the shock of Granny dying and the other business about the bombers, but now she found herself gazing down as though her son were . . . no, not even a stranger, because other people's babies could give you a bit of that sort of kick, and so could kittens and foals . . . but a specimen, an exhibit. Vertebrate, mammal, ape, human, infant, royal. Louise was alien as a guardian angel watching over the cot in perfect but emotionless duty. She felt outside herself, outside time. Time, in fact, displayed itself in front of her mind's eye like the replica of the Bayeux Tapestry which stood at the end of an upper corridor in the Palace, the whole darned thing on a strip of canvas wound onto a pair of rollers so that you could trundle the strip forward or back with an electric motor.

During last night time had trundled. The pictures had moved. A generation had gone (not quite, because Aunt Tim York was still puttering quietly on, but that bit of the Family had got out of synch so that at one time there'd been gossip about Louise marrying Cousin Jack, who really belonged in Father's generation). Granny and her harp and dyed hair and crazy clothes had been wound out of sight, leaving Mother and Father on the left of the picture now, in the middle Albert and Soppy, Louise and Piers, on the right Albert's two kids, and last of all, wound into view only a few weeks back, this cartoon baby in his cartoon cot. DAVIDUS NATUS EST said the clumsy letters above.

In the bedroom the telephone rang. Louise reached for the intercom and switched it through.

"Joan? You heard the news?"

"I'm sorry, ma'am."

"It's all right. No one's going to miss her much, except Aunt Bea."

"Yes, I know. Still . . . I was calling to know if you'd like me down early."

"Late, if anything. Let's all have a lie-in. I should think the Visiting Head's off, as far as I'm concerned. The Palace will be ringing with the Guidance around ten — we'll have a skim through the diaries and see if there's anything we want to make a fuss about. Father says Thursday week for the funeral."

"Right."

"See you around nine, then. Sleep well."

At the click of the intercom Davy's smooth forehead wrinkled then cleared. The clenched hand loosed itself, the ridiculous little fingers probed blindly at the mattress. A

13

dream, just before waking, brief, but leaving the face changed when it ended. It wasn't the sort of change you could measure or point at but it was there. Louise recognised the look at once. Davy's visible eye was closed, his nose was a mere blob, his hair dark fluff, but his look was Granny.

She bent and lifted him free. Still asleep he snuggled against her, fitting himself to her body like a piece of some soft jigsaw which belonged there and nowhere else in the universe. By the time she had stripped away his reeking nappies and padded him dry his lips were pouting into sucks. Deeply contented, with the drug of motherhood now flooding through her veins, she carried the last of the Romanovs back to her bed to feed.

3

As always, they lay in the dark and talked. It was already so much of a habit that when they had to spend a night apart Louise found that she needed to hold an imaginary conversation, muttering her own lines into the stillness, before she could happily fall asleep.

" . . . it was quite peculiar. Do you believe in reincarnation? He looked just like her for a few seconds."

"You think he's been on hold until your grandmother's soul was free to take over?"

"It makes a change from looking like Queen Victoria. Half the babies you see look like her. But you get these sort of flickers. You can see there's a likeness but you don't know who. One of yours, I suppose."

"Post-natal recapitulation. The foetus in the womb recapitulates the stages of human evolution. First it's an amoeba, later it has gills, then it's an amphibian and so on. Shortly before birth it has traces of a simian tail. Why should the process stop there?"

"We were monkeys for much longer than Granny was Granny."

"I'm not suggesting Davy was recapitulating your grandmother. Suppose a period in prehistory when various human groups became largely segregated, with the result that particular characteristics tended to be bred into one group and not another, and then to remain as part of our genetic material. Sometimes they would emerge in a life-long likeness, as in your grandmother, but with the majority of descendants they wouldn't manifest themselves except for the brief period in which the child was recapitulating that stage of its evolution."

"Is that genuine science?"

"Just doodling. I could ask someone, if you like."

"I just love the idea of a pack of Romanovs wearing nothing except mink and sable hunter-gathering across the steppes for Fabergé eggs!"

"More engaging to contemplate than to encounter."

"I bet you Granny would have come out on top if she'd been one of them."

NOVEMBER 1987

I

"*That you?*"

"*. . .*"

"*Well?*"

"*. . .*"

"*What do you mean, pressure?*"

"*. . .*"

"*Tell me this — supposing I went along with you, does it mean nobody getting hurt or killed?*"

"*. . .*"

"*It's what matters to me — that and saving your stupid skin.*"

"*. . .*"

"*And you can't say more? Anyway, it'd be down to me to come up with something, wouldn't it?*"

"*. . .*"

"*All right. I'm not saying I like it, but I'll give it a try. But listen, there's your side of the bargain. You're going to promise me, whatever happens, soon as this is over you're getting out. And you're not getting involved in anything else like this, ever again. Right?*"

"*. . .*"

2

It was part of our unwritten constitution, Father used to say, that there must always be one UMRF — Unpopular Member of Royal Family. Granny had held the office for more than a generation. It had certain perks, the best being certain freedoms from constraint experienced by those members of the

Family who were expected to behave; now, finally, there was freedom from TV at her funeral. This gave the service a feeling of taking place back in the 'thirties, when all the public would have expected to see was a double-page spread in the *Illustrated London News*, drawn by an artist who had not been present at the ceremony. Granny had of course been born Russian Orthodox but she'd had to become C of E in order to marry Grandfather, so the spoken bits of the service were good old Prayer Book. For the music they'd got St Paul's and Westminster Abbey to lend them extra basses who boomed away in furry deep voices trying to sound like Chaliapin. To Louise this seemed a much more agreeable noise than the flutings and twitterings she usually had to sit through.

There was a good turn-out of Romanovs. The Palace were always jumpy about any dealings with Russian ex-royals, partly because of their experiences with Granny but mainly because the FO would come at them with tut-tuts if it seemed that any Romanov was being treated in a way which implied that he was still really royal and might one day come into his own again. For instance there was only to be a buffet luncheon after the ceremony, so that nobody could say that the King of England had sat down to a formal meal with a claimant to the throne of the Tsars. Louise knew only three of the visitors by sight, so whiled away the musical stretches by studying the rest of them for Davy-likenesses and any other evidence of Romanov hunter-gatherer forebears. Beyond a vague foreignness she could detect no special shared traits among the men, but four of the women were striking in the same fashion, erect, pale-skinned and dark-haired, with strong-featured square faces — the famous Bagration look of which Granny used to boast not because she herself possessed it but because it came from the oldest royal line in Europe.

The home-growns had come in force, almost the complete set: Granny's own children apart from Aunt Louise, who'd refused to make the trip from Rome — she'd always hated Granny, Father said, with a sort of phobia quite different from what he regarded as his own rational detestation — Father and Mother, Uncle Billy and the Clarences, Aunt Anne and Uncle Boot Wroxeter and the Wroxeter cousins; the grandchildren, of course; and then the outer ring of second cousins, the Yorks and the Kents and their ramifications, complicated by divorces and re-marriages — and not one of them caring a sausage that Granny had snuffed it at last. In all that solemn and apparently mourning assembly only Aunt Bea Surbiton could be feeling genuine sorrow, though perhaps a few others might share Louise's mild regret — not that even she had actually liked Granny, but she had at times enjoyed her, her gusto, her panache, her irreverence (especially of all things that the English expected one to revere), her undauntedness in accepting her unpopularity and making the most of it, wearing it like one of her absurd gaudy cloaks and flaunting it in the face of her enemies. Granny had been a flavour in Louise's growing up. You didn't want much of it, and not often, but from now on you were going to taste it only in memory.

A bout of Slavic boomings ended. The organ took up with burps and tootles. The coffin-bearers — chosen from the regiments of which Granny had been Colonel-in-Chief, a rank she had relished exploiting to the maximum of military embarrassment — hefted the box and waited. Louise rose when Mother rose and leaving Piers in his stall joined the procession beside Albert, who was looking peculiarly kempt and respectable. He had been tending that way for some while, his beard seeming to have become smaller and neater every time Louise met him — perhaps Soppy kept a pair of scissors under her pillow and snipped another millimetre away each night while he slept. The procession caterpillared to the vault. The organ whumped, fluttered and fell silent. The Dean turned and raised his head with a look of astonishment, as though he had imagined he had been wandering alone through an empty chapel, and now found that he had been trailing an entire royal family behind him. He drew a deep breath and twanged through his nose, till the choir drowned him with hootings and flutings.

"Man that is born of woman . . ."

". . . hath but a short time to live and is full of misery. He cometh up and is cut down like a flower . . ."

And jumpeth off pianos trying to catch parrots, thought Louise as the soldiers eased the coffin onto the platform that would carry it down into the vault. It settled without a bump.

The machinery took over. The supernumerary basses rumbled fresh woe. Slowly the box slid away.

"Made it," whispered Albert.

There had been suggestions in the press, as well as private chunterings among Palace officials, that Granny shouldn't be buried in St George's. It wasn't just that she'd never been Queen. Her known Nazi sympathies, both before and during the war, were the main thing, but she had plenty of enemies from other causes who would have liked to see her buried less triumphally. Mother could well have been chief of those enemies, since Granny had set out from the start to make life as tricky as possible for the new Queen, but of course it had been Mother who had insisted that Granny must be buried alongside poor Grandfather.

Louise agreed. After all, he'd really loved her. There were only two things everybody knew about Grandfather. One was his managing to set fire to his yacht during a practical joke with an exploding cigar and so getting drowned in a flat calm sea while he was still only Prince of Wales — extraordinary to think of a time when you could go yachting with a few cronies and not have posses of security men zooming all round you in power boats and helicopters. The other was that he'd really loved Granny. Mother and Father loved each other, of course, both officially and unofficially; they'd just had a bit of a fight to get married, too. Louise herself was known to be dotty about Piers, and had had to fight even harder. But if you'd asked your woman-in-the-checkout-queue to name you a royal romance, three times out of four she's still have answered "Oh, poor Prince Albert and the Grand Duchess." She'd have been right, too, despite the fact that Granny was capable of conducting a world-class romance without really loving the other party much more than she loved her harp or her jewellery. She would have seen the lover mainly as an extension of her own personality. But Grandfather'd never had the imagination for that. He'd loved her and fought to marry her against his parents and the government, the Church, the hacks, and practically the whole of the Great British Public — even greater odds than Louise had faced for Piers. And then the GBP, like a tyranni-cal father in a costume drama, had suddenly recognised True

Love and changed sides, so Grandfather had won. It was the only noticeable thing he'd ever done, really, but it was enough. Then he'd drowned, and fifty years of widowhood had juddered by, and now she was sliding down to sleep by her husband's side again.

Marriage is rum, Louise thought. All marriages, not just the slightly peculiar ones like Father's with Mother and Nonny. She didn't think she'd really considered this before. Getting used to Piers's peculiarities and finding ways of living together, as well as setting up house and having a baby, had been a mind-absorbing process, as inevitable as time seems to the time-bound. But now Granny, was drifting away to somewhere outside time, and seemed for a moment to be sucking Louise in her wake, enabling her not only to look at her memories but also at the possible lifetimes ahead, and feel the same strangeness in them all. She couldn't find words for the feeling. It didn't have much to do with love — love just made it all harder to think about. If Piers had been at her side she would have felt for his hand and he would have squeezed hers without seeming to notice what he was doing, but afterwards he would have asked "What was that about?" and she would have said "Oh nothing." When she slid back into time she felt widowed.

She shook herself. A boy was singing solo in those blood-less, floating tones which always gave Louise the illusion that if only she could dissolve one flimsy barrier between her ear and her mind she might be able to grasp why people made such a fuss about music.

". . . is not at our last hour for any pains of death to fall from Thee."

Father stepped forward. Somebody offered him an urn from which he took a handful of dry earth.

"For as much as it hath pleased Almighty God," twanged the Dean, "of His great mercy to take unto Himself the soul of our dear sister here departed . . ."

Father tossed the earth down. It rattled like rain among the wreaths that covered the vanishing coffin. The Dean pro-longed his last twang into a dying whine. The Family turned, processed back and peeled off to their places. Piers, un-prompted, felt for Louise's hand and squeezed it.

The Princess of Wales — Sophia on her birth certificate, Sophie to the hacks, Soppy to anyone who knew her well — was standing by a window that looked out over the Home Park. The view was silver and brown and gold, pale clouds reflected from the ponds, withering grass-stems littered with yellow leaf-fall, all hues muted still further by the remains of mist, as though seen on TV with the colour-control down. Two of the best trees had fallen in the famous gale, their prone trunks adding to the melancholy. It was all very pallid, peaceful, English, nothing like Granny. Soppy as usual had been first to the tables and her plate had an Alp of food on it.

"How's life?" said Louise.

"Sacked my Bridget yesterday."

"Oh, why? I thought she was terrific."

"Got on my nerves. Don't talk to Bertie about it. He's far from chuffed. Still like that wench of yours?"

"Janine? I was thinking, oh, the morning after Granny died, how super she was. I keep finding her up and there when it's not even her night on. Luckily Davy's just beginning to sleep through, touch wood."

"Mercy when that happens. Watching anyone else feed makes my tummy rumble. My two must've got conditioned to the idea of distant thunder with their meals — won't be able to digest without it. Tried keeping a few snacks my side of the bed, but Bertie complained about the crumbs."

"I was thinking how tidied-up you're getting him."

"Not me, darling. People change. Closer you think you are to them, less you notice. Then all of a sudden you've got someone else."

Soppy popped a whole canapé into her neat round mouth and chewed double-speed, wrinkling her nose as she did so. She had an unusually small head with sharp little features and slightly pop eyes. Her body was long but neat, unaffected by her astounding appetite. She was said to be the best woman polo-player in Europe. Louise liked her, but she was not very popular with the Palace because of her tendency to say things they hadn't scripted.

"Piers says we aren't just one person like that, really," said Louise.

"Uh?"

"Don't tell him I've told you. He says I always make things simpler than they are, especially anything to do with AI."

"Trying to get computers to think for themselves, I tell people. Heard Uncle Boot ask him what was the point and Piers said he didn't guarantee a point. Very Piers. Quite a bit going on, I gather."

"Lots, and all beyond me. Piers's line is trying to get the brutes to evolve a bit of intelligence for themselves."

"Take him a few million years, won't it? Did us."

"He's not going that far. I only said 'a bit'. He doesn't want to evolve the whole shoot — in fact he says we didn't either. We evolved bits too, to cope with different sorts of things, and then lumped them together. He says I'm not really one person having one lot of thoughts and feelings, like I think I am. Really I'm a sort of committee, different bits of me politicking and squabbling away and then coming out with a sort of agreed statement and then I say to myself 'That's what I think' which makes me think there's a whole me thinking it. We've got to think like that or we'd go potty."

Louise realised that Soppy had stopped listening in order to gobble with yet more concentrated ferocity.

"Are you having problems with Bertie?" she murmured.

"No."

Soppy had answered automatically and was about to shovel another forkful in when she seemed to pull herself up. Her eyes flickered over Louise's shoulder. Louise had herself glanced into the pier-glass between the windows before she had asked the question. It was all automatic, not that you knew there were people in the room who were likely to pass the gossip directly on to the hacks, but less obvious lines of communication — Aunt Eloise Kent hinting to a crony, the crony tattling to her chiropodist — lay always waiting, like the tentacles of a sea anemone poised in their pool for scraps. Soppy popped the fork-load in but munched more slowly, apparently thinking how much to say.

"It's not Bertie", she said. "I mean, yes it is, but not like that. Hasn't got a girl, far as I know, still expects a good bit of action in bed. Anyway, it isn't just him. He's different, I'm different, everything's different."

"Have you talked to him about it?"

"Wouldn't know what to say. Scared of burning my boats. See a psychiatrist, d'you think?"

"They say it isn't much use unless you actually want to."

"Don't. Anyway, I'm too young to go potty. Auntie Kitty was pushing sixty. Got any plans for that bit of duck? Thanks."

Louise let her plate be raided. Soppy sounded more than a bit miserable, curiously ashamed and scared. Her great-aunt, Lady Kitty Bakewell, had gone round the bend about the time Louise was born and had barricaded herself into the stable flat at Coryon and, with the help of her butler and a pair of shotguns, had held out for several days. She'd still been alive when Albert's engagement to Soppy had been announced, and hacks had actually broken into the home where she was kept and tried to interview her. Other hacks had speculated on the possibility that the madness ran in the family. It had all been fairly typically unpleasant, not helped by the fact that there was something a little odd-looking about Soppy, something out-of-proportion, which came out in certain pictures, though in others she simply looked like the GBP's dream, the doll princess.

"Would it help if I talked to Bertie?" said Louise. "I wouldn't say anything direct."

Soppy shrugged.

"Probably just the time of year," she said. "Always used to look forward to it. Skipped the whole grisly Christmas hoo-ha by nipping off to the Argentine for a couple of months."

"Two months, and no diary at all!"

"Just polo."

"Bliss!"

"I've managed to clear a fortnight in Feb. That's the lot."

"But they won't let you go there, will they? I . . . "

"Course not. Florida."

"They play polo there?"

"Pretty good. But . . . Hell, I don't see why I can't go to the Argentine if I want. I didn't start the bloody war. I don't care a hoot what happens to the bloody Falklands. They don't belong to us. Never did."

23

Soppy's voice was begining to rise. If any of the anemone's tentacles were floating near by, they'd be beginning to sense the presence of a titbit.

"It's just one of those things," said Louise in a deliberately deadening tone.

"Ta ever so, darling. Second help? I'm going to. Talk to Bertie if you want — better not try and tell me what he says."

Albert in fact was only a group away, listening to his mother-in-law, Aunt Eloise Kent, who was the obvious next candidate for the title of UMRF, though earning it in a different style from Granny, coldly self-willed, power-hungry and devious. Louise couldn't imagine herself tolerating, let alone half-liking Aunt Eloise the way she had Granny, nor was this a possible moment to tackle Albert, so she drifted herself in the other direction, theoretically looking for some cousin or guest who seemed left-out, but knowing that the drift would continue till she fetched up alongside Piers. She found him by the fire, of course, scorching his hams while he talked to a stranger. They made a joke pair, the stranger small and shiny and round, bobbing continually on the balls of his feet like a balloon at a souvenir stall, and Piers bending over him with the vulture look he wore when amused or interested. In his funeral black Piers could easily have been mistaken for an undertaker's assistant who had been misdirected into the gathering and was making the best of the free meal. (He claimed to prefer beer to wine, but his glass seldom stayed full of either for long; he ate nearly as much as Soppy.)

"Hello, darling," he said. "Have you met Alex Romanov? Prince, is it?"

"For today Count, I suppose," said the stranger. "Usually plain Doctor. Your Highness."

He got it exactly right, the small bow, the touch of the hand, the accepting tone of voice. His eyes were bright with fun. He gave the instant impression that he expected to enjoy your company.

"A proper doctoring doctor?" said Louise.

"A philosophising doctor. They never told me it was improper."

24

"We're in the same line," said Piers. "Only Alex has gone where the loot is. Expert systems."

"Then I'll push off and leave you at it," said Louise.

"Oh, please not, ma'am, " said Count Alex. "Lord Chandler and I can get together any time, but I may not have another chance to talk to somebody who knew the Grand Duchess well."

"I didn't think you Romanovs agreed she was one."

(Granny's claim to the title had been part of her general campaign of making people realise that for her marrying into the British royal family had been a come-down.)

"In my eyes she was above technicalities," said Count Alex.

"You're the only two I've met who had a good word to say for the old girl," said Piers.

"I met her just once," said Count Alex. "When I was seven. I was taken by my mother for inspection. She wore more rings that I have ever seen on one hand and stuffed my mouth with small sweet cakes as though I'd been a dog."

"Trying to make you sick," said Louise. "She did that."

"At the same time she said cruel little things to my mother. I didn't understand them, but I could feel the cruelty and was intrigued, and often asked when we could go again. At Epiphany, with the help of my nurse — I had so many nurses and governesses, but almost all of them I contrived to make allies against my mother — I sent the Grand Duchess a card. I didn't know how to make Russian letters but I used Russian words. She must have been amused, for she replied."

"No! In that terrible green ink?"

"Being a child I took it for granted. She wrote in green ink at first, but later changed to a pale, hard pencil."

"You mean she kept it up! She never wrote to anyone if she could help it. The telephone was a way of life to her."

"Not in my case. I found out when her birthday was and wrote again, but she didn't answer. Next year I tried once more. There'd been some rumpus among the cousins and I told her about it, for something to say, and this time she replied telling me that she had enjoyed my letter and if I heard similar stories I must let her know. We are an unimportant branch of the family, but my mother had made it her business to become a sort of nodal point in the network. She did not create scandal, but she processed it and passed it on. I would lie on my stomach and draw in my book and listen, and whenever I heard of one of the cousins doing something characteristic I'd tell myself 'That might amuse the Grand Duchess,' and send her a letter. After a while she began to reciprocate. We always wrote in Russian, so it was quite safe, but I know more about your family than you might think, ma'am."

He beamed. Louise smiled back, relying on a lifetime of face-control. Did he really not understand what he was telling her?

"Granny wasn't all that reliable," she said. "I mean she once told me my grandfather was drowned by the secret service on orders from Lord Halifax to prevent her from becoming Queen and making friends with Hitler and stopping the Second World War."

Count Alex nodded. That must be in the letters.

"Oh, there's a lot of noise," he said.

"Almost white in her case," said Piers.

"Yes, white Russian noise," said Count Alex.

"You're leaving me out," said Louise.

"Noise is gibberish from which one attempts to extract a signal," said Piers. "White noise is pure random gibberish."

"Yes, of course," said Count Alex. "It was a curious relationship. She let me understand quite soon that she had no wish to see me again. At first I suspect that she may have been mainly concerned to create mischief for my mother, but if so she misunderstood the relationship, which was . . . let's not go into that. Later, when she appreciated how well-placed I was to keep her *au fait* with *émigré* affairs, she used me for that, and also as a repository for some of her own spites and spleens. I agree with what you say about her unreliability, but it wasn't total. Sometimes she would comment on what I had told her and add anecdotes about previous Romanov scandals which I was able to check. The facts she seldom did more than embroider. It was her interpretation of the facts which was grotesque."

"Have you talked to Aunt Bea? Lady Surbiton, you know?"

Count Alex laughed aloud.

"She is a figure of myth to me," he said. "The Grand Duchess's letters always ended with a postscript describing her latest persecution of poor Lady Surbiton. She claimed it was necessary to keep Lady Surbiton's bowels open. Yet I gather Lady Surbiton was devoted to her."

"She's heartbroken," said Louise.

"It must have been like one of those marriages — the sort where no one on the outside can understand how the couple make it work."

"All marriages are of that nature," said Piers.

"Except the ones which really don't work," said Louise. "Come and find Aunt Bea. She's getting a bit deaf these days."

"How very extraordinary," said Aunt Bea in her breathy near-whisper. "I had no idea. Of course HRH could be peculiarly secretive."

She sighed. Mother had settled her on a *chaise longue* and arranged a rota of the family to cheer her up, but none of them had achieved much, Louise guessed, until Count Alex settled beside her and started to talk, apparently focussing the whole of his bubbling attention on Aunt Bea's soft, white, grief-dulled countenance. Louise was impressed. Most new-comers would have shown at least disguised reluctance to be transferred from talk with a newsworthy princess to a dull ex-lady-in-waiting. She was threading her way back towards Piers when her path was blocked by Father's private secretary, Sir Savile Tendence. His attempt to stand aside was hampered by the three plates of walnut meringue he was balancing on one arm and the several brimming glasses in the other hand. He smiled his controlled tired smile.

"Hello, Sir Sam," said Louise. "When you get sick of us you can always get a job as a juggler's mate."

"I shall come to you for a reference, ma'am. Impressive little ceremony the kontakion made it, don't you think? Life's going to be quieter without her."

"Don't you believe it. She'll make a pretty effective ghost. Uncanny harp-twangings at the wrong moment. Where did you find Count Alex Romanov?"

"The little shiny one? We didn't find him. HRH left instructions that he was to be invited to the funeral. He is named in her will as literary executor — not a very onerous responsibility, one would think, with just that monograph on the harp. Presumably he has an interest in things musical."

"I don't know. He says they were pen-pals. He's still got a lot of her letters. They used to send each other family gossip."

Sir Savile had already been on the move with his teetering load. He stopped.

"*Our* family?" he murmured.

"Yes."

"Dear me."

"He says he doesn't necessarily believe everything she told him."

"Oh, it wouldn't need to be *true*. Has he any idea what he's got there, d'you imagine?"

Louise considered. People, especially intelligent ones, could be extraordinarily naive about what mattered once you became involved with the Family, but Count Alex had given the impression of being fully aware of the nuances around him. You wouldn't be much good as a gossip-relay if you weren't.

"Yes, probably," she said.

"Dear me."

"They're all in Russian."

"I suppose that's something. I'd better have a word with HM. How did you run into the chap? I mean, did he come beavering over to you to tell you?"

"No. He was talking to Piers about AI, and then when I showed up he got on to the letters."

"AI?"

"Artificial Intelligence."

"Is there any other kind?"

"It's Count Alex's job too."

"Is it, now? Perhaps you might suggest to Lord Chandler that he keeps in touch, hm?"

"They seemed to be getting on. Tell Father to ring me if he wants to know any more."

Sir Savile moved away but before Louise could do so too

she felt a touch on her elbow and turned to find it was Albert.

"Got a moment?" he said. "Not in here. Shouldn't be anyone in the Stamp Room."

"I'll just tell Piers."

Great-grandfather, King Victor I, had been a man of few interests. He shot and went racing, because he was expected to. He played simple card-games for large stakes, and snooker. His rumoured youthful enthusiasms were not permissible under the steely rule of Great-grandmama. But somebody must have decided that a monarch ought to be publicly known to have concerns of a vaguely intellectual kind, and that in King Victor's case philately was about the highest level he could plausibly be represented as having attained. The Royal Stamp Collection was housed in a small room off the State Apartments, not much changed since King Victor's day, with its pair of reading-desks and its low leather arm-chairs in which a man might relax with his Hine and Havana after the effort of studying an 1866 Bolivian five-centavo mauve. Louise found Albert already in one of the chairs, in exactly the right pose, slumped back with his wine-glass in his hand. It was a mild shock; despite having thought about his new neatness at the funeral, and what Soppy had said about his having changed, Louise's mental image of her elder brother was still that of a few years back, the hairy leftie vegetarian who harangued banquets of financiers about the vital need to preserve the habitat of the natterjack toad. Now, in his formal clothes, with his beard trimmed to a naval wedge and his hair receding sharply above the temples, he could have been the ghost of Great-grandfather, apart from the blue intelligent gaze.

"You'll be eating veal next," said Louise.

He twitched his head, puzzled. Her skirt was too tight to copy his pose so she perched on a chair-wing.

"You've changed," she said.

"Have I? Doesn't feel like that, from inside — I suppose it never does. You were talking to Soppy."

"Nice to see her."

"What did you think?"

"She seemed a bit down."

"Understatement of the year. She's pretty well at the end of her tether. So, if it comes to that, am I."

"I was just thinking how smug and kempt you look."

"Training."

"Isn't it just the time of year? Christmases with Aunt Eloise must have been pretty good hell. Soppy says she used to get out of it by nipping off to Argentina, but I don't think you get away from your childhood that easy."

"I tried to get her out there this year. I thought there might be a chance, with the FO wanting to pretend the Falklands War was only a sort of folk-myth which never really happened at all, but Mrs T. put her foot down. Don't you long for the days when you could go buzzing around the world incognito and everyone looked the other way?"

"The hacks would make a real meal of her, I suppose."

"She's not been coping with the hacks that well, actually. I don't know. She knew what she was in for when she took me on, I thought."

"You don't. No one does. I was brooding about Granny's marriage. No one else can imagine what it's like, and no one can imagine what their own one's going to be like."

"Anyway, it isn't just the hacks. Did she tell you she'd sacked poor Bridget while I was in Oslo, for no reason she can explain? Just said the girl got on her nerves."

"It happens."

"Not like that. I tried to reason with her and she clammed up. She's eating much too much."

Louise just stopped the burst of laughter. How could he tell? Soppy's appetite was known to be limitless. It had been a family joke since nursery days. But she could see that Albert had taken that into account and was still bothered.

"You saw what she had on her plate?" he said. "She'll fill it up a couple of times, and then she'll do her duty by three or four puddings and top off with a few slabs of cheese — and then as soon as we're home she'll be at the fridge for a snack."

"She ought to be in *The Guinness Book of Records*."

"They wouldn't let her in. She cheats. She's taking pills to help shove it through."

"Oh. I must say that doesn't sound too good."

"No. Any ideas?"

"Well . . . I think she's bothered, too. I said something about how spruce you were getting to look and she started talking about how everybody was different . . . Do you still love her, Bert?"

Albert protected himself from any direct display of emotion by going into his Father-imitation, poising the tips of his fingers together and giving a snort through his moustache.

"Trick question," he said. "When did you stop loving your wife? I love her OK, but in a different way from a few years back. Much more complex. I mean, for instance, it includes a good deal of irritation sometimes. It's like, oh well, for instance, the shift from the intense simplicities of folk music to the interwoven diffusions of polyphony, if you follow me."

"I don't."

"Sorry. I forgot. Well, then, it's like coming off the high moorlands where you can see for miles and there isn't a soul in sight and the winds of heaven to breathe, to walking through close farmland with hedges and twisting lanes and business calls to make on the way."

"That's more like it. Perhaps Soppy's hankering for the hill-tops."

"You can't stay there for ever, but monogamy still rules in my case, if that's what you mean. That wasn't why she sacked Bridget. I don't think that's the problem. For instance, she found an old snap of Aunt Kitty Bakewell in her twenties, long before she showed any sign of going off her trolley, dolled up as a man for some kind of fancy dress do in a white tie and tails and looking stunning. First glance you'd think it was Soppy herself. And she keeps dragging Kitty into con-versations — not right in, just hinting and then pushing her out of sight again."

"Soppy's always looked terrific in uniform. Piers is mad about her."

"Piers is just kinky about women in uniform. Look how he got Mother to dress up in her Irish Guards outfit last Christ-mas. To my mind it all goes back to his being found on that bus. His mother must have been some buxom conductress, and he's working out his pre-natal influences."

"Seriously?"

"No. Of course not. But I'm serious about Soppy. I think her problems are mostly down to Aunt Eloise."

"Do you really? Soppy always gives the impression of being the only one who can handle her."

"As she grew up she evolved various strategies and techniques, but she wouldn't have had them when she was a child. All it means is that everything's deeper-buried, hidden from her conscious mind, so she has to blame her problems on things that are happening to her now, like not being allowed to go to Argentina. I don't know what it is about some people's mothers."

"At least we've been lucky with our own. Did you meet Alex Romanov? His was a handful too, by the sound of her. You might've noticed me taking him over to woo poor Aunt Bea."

"Oh, him . . . looked as if he was making a go of it, too. Where did you pick him up?"

"He was talking to Piers about AI. He used to correspond with Granny on a regular basis, he says. He's got a lot of her letters, long ones, full of the sort of things she used to say about everyone."

"Has he, by God? That's what you were telling Sir Sam? No wonder he looked a bit haunted. What's he going to do?"

"Try and con them off him somehow, I should think."

"Why bother?"

Louise stared. It seemed too obvious to argue about. There was no question of the Palace allowing Granny's papers to be published as they stood. Even letting Alex Romanov get as far as trying to publish them, and then having to go to the courts to get them suppressed, would wake an absolute volcano of guesswork and rumour about what might be in them.

"You know what I think?" said Albert. "Seriously. The best way to deal with a time-bomb like this is blow it up in the open. We should help Mr Romanov get the stuff published."

"Count. Or Doctor. You did say 'Seriously'?"

"Father writes a pious foreword. That gives the Palace a bit of a say, and Sir Sam can blue-pencil the iffy bits."

32

"It's all going to be iffy in Sir Sam's eyes."

"Time he went."

Albert had spoken casually, as if adding a footnote to the conversation. Louise looked at him. He shrugged. The gesture, allied to the slumped, clubland pose, had a masculine ruthlessness about it which Louise found hard to associate with the Albert she had known all her life until they had moved into their separating marriages. Sir Savile seemed a large and unchanging object in her mental landscape, single-mindedly loyal, according to his lights. Now, in Albert's eyes, it was time that bit of landscape was cleared. Soppy was right. Albert had changed in aspects less obvious than the cut of his beard.

"Is there anything you'd like me to do about Soppy?" she said. "I could try and get her to talk if you want. I don't think it would be much use just telling her to cut down on the calories."

"No, of course not. I wanted to know what you thought, and talk about her a bit. There's no one else, so I'm afraid you've got to bear with it."

"All I can suggest is you might try getting back up on the hill-tops a bit. Perhaps she isn't ready for ordinary country walks all the time. I know it's difficult — no use if you're faking it. Couldn't you set up some kind of escapade, something that really felt like a break-out ... I don't know, smuggle her out to Argentina in a false nose and then arrange to turn up yourself, unbeknownst to her. She canters across at the end of the second chukka and there you are holding her remount."

Albert laughed, then sighed.

"You remember how we used to fantasise about what they could do to us?" said Louise. "Putting us in the Tower, and us appealing to the European Court of Human Rights? I mean, how would they physically stop you ...?"

"You're not helping, Lulu."

"Sorry. I know."

"My fault. I oughtn't to have bothered you."

"I really want to help. I like Soppy a lot, for one thing. So does Piers. Can I talk to him?"

"If you want to. I suppose he's got an angle on what some

33

of it's like which we can't have. What I'd like is next time she starts hinting about Aunt Kitty I'll see if I can't persuade her to talk to a psychiatrist, just to set her mind at rest. Then if she gets on with him . . ."

"Her," said Louise.

"Oh. Right. I'll ask around. Time we were getting back?" They rose.

"Thanks," he said. "You mayn't think it, but that's helped a bit."

"Any time. It matters more than most things."

"I know. Had I better take a squint at your Romanov friend? You never said what you made of him."

"He's got a lot of charm. It's real. It was there for Aunt Bea, too."

"Talked to any of the others? They strike me as a rum lot."

"I was thinking about Granny. You know, she wasn't really civilised. I wouldn't have put anything past her."

"Right."

3

" . . . I thought we might be seeing him again anyway," said Piers. "It's not that often we bump into a chap who can get along in both our languages."

"Let's have a supper in your flat. You can ask the Stokeses and Isabelle. Tracy and I can talk obstetrics while you four zoom around on the higher plane."

"If you like."

"I'll get Joan to find a hole in the diary. Not too soon, or Alex might smell a rat."

"It's you and your lot who are doing the rat-smelling, in my opinion. Alex struck me as a decent enough bloke."

"I thought so too, what I saw of him. You've got to expect us to be jumpy about Romanovs. Even leaving Granny out they're an odd lot. There've been some terrific scandals."

"Would you say that an excessive sense of personal honour was an hereditary characteristic in them?"

(Piers, as usual when bed-talk turned to the Family, was trying to distance himself by adopting the tone and phrase-

34

ology of the sort of don who must have been pretty well extinct even in his student days.)

"I don't know. Granny was the only one I knew well. When it suited her, I suppose . . . Why?"

"One could conceive of Alex deciding that since your grandmother entrusted him with her letters partly in the hope that he would use them to continue her various feuds after her death, he might regard it as his duty to do so."

"And there'd be quite a bit of money in it, too. Anyway, could he? How much is a literary executor allowed to do? If the family don't want it, I mean?"

"It would depend on the wording of the will, I imagine. In any case Sir Savile's office will presumably exhume some pre-Reformation statute in Norman French which empowers your father to have any subjects disembowelled who attempt to publish his mother's correspondence against his will."

"I can just see the headlines. That's the whole point, darling. There'll be almost more fuss if it gets out we're trying to put the lid on things than if we let it all come out. And it doesn't make any difference that Granny will have got it all wrong. Look at the poor old Dingwalls."

(When, on the announcement of Louise's engagement to Piers, the hacks had discovered that on the groom's side no family at all existed to be harried for childhood memories, incredible efforts had been made to excavate a hidden past. The search itself had become its own news. One line had been to hunt up doubles of the new celebrity, especially in the neighbourhood of Coventry. A foreman of an abattoir had been found living at Leamington Spa who had a definite resemblance, so his parents — the father had also been in the meat trade — had had to put up not only with several weeks' ferocious scrutiny but with a series of "revelations", all foundationless, about one or other of them having a secret in their past, once shameful but now in the eyes of the hacks glorious beyond belief.)

"You realise that if Alex is motivated as Sir Savile seems to fear, inviting him to supper may be interpreted by him as meaning that he has hooked his fish?"

"He has, hasn't he? If he's fishing. But if he is then someone's going to have to talk to him somehow, and if he isn't we'll just have had a nice supper-party."

"Sir Savile could send some pin-striped emissary."

"Father's always dead against that, if he can help it. Next thing you know is Security have got in on the act and his phone's being tapped and someone's faked a burglary and gone through his papers, and then you've got questions in the House and there's hell to pay. Perhaps I oughtn't to have told Sir Sam in the first place."

"I'd have imagined Security had enough on their plates preventing us from living our own lives the way we want to."

"It won't last much longer, darling. It's just another scare. They'll find Gorman's brother living it up under an assumed name in New Orleans, or something. It'll blow over. They always do."

NOVEMBER/DECEMBER 1987

I

"That you?"

" . . . "

"Now listen carefully. I've got something, might do. Got a pencil and paper?"

" . . . "

"There's someone called Alex Romanov — don't know how you spell it but it's the same as the Russian royal family used to be. Don't know his address. The point is, he's got hold of a lot of letters the old Dowager Princess wrote, the one who had the funeral last week. They're full of all kinds of dirt about the royals. What I was thinking is, suppose you could get a line on him . . . "

2

Choosing Christmas presents was another thing that had quietly changed its nature over recent years. Inevitably, as it swelled and swelled, the Duty List had had to be standardised — so many hampers from Fortnum's, bottles from Berry Bros, soft toys from Hamleys, all the way down to tights from Marks and Sparks. Joan took care of that, and Louise started signing the cards in September. But even choosing things for the Family, which of course she did herself, was no longer the fun it used to be; not living among them now she lacked the confidence of rightness she needed in matching present to person. For instance, a colleague of Piers had set up a three-man company in the Industrial Park attached to the university to make and market gadgets and toys he had invented as a by-product of his research. The fancy intercom

37

Louise used in the nursery was a prototype of his, and this
year he had come up with a sort of magician's wand you
could point at any light-fitting in a room and make it change
intensity or colour. The toy needed special light-fittings, of
course, and was about three times as expensive as Mother
would have approved of, but it felt perfect for Father — or
would have, two Christmases ago. It probably still was, but
Louise didn't feel the same certainty and inward satisfaction
that she would have in the old days. Perhaps Father had
changed, like Albert. Would Albert really be pleased with his
weaver-birds? And so on. Even Aunt Bea . . .

Louise had always given Aunt Bea a huge jigsaw which she
took about three months to piece together and then passed on
to a hospital. She was strangely puritanical about it, refusing
to look at the picture on the lid but letting it gradually reveal
itself as she nudged the pieces around with her pudgy white
hands, trying and sighing. It was hard to say how much
pleasure she got out of the task, in fact it seemed more like
some sort of mystical exercise she was forced to perform as
part of her duties, bringing into the world images that had
hitherto existed only in a royal mind. Louise wanted the
picture to be worth the trouble so, though she could easily
have asked Joan to tell Hamleys to send a big puzzle while she
was ordering the teddy-bears, she preferred to choose it
herself. Only after doing so — it was a Lowry snowscape,
with soaring factory chimneys and the usual matchstick
figures — did it occur to her to wonder whether Aunt Bea
would still be interested.

Though it was still four weeks till Christmas she decided
on impulse to deliver it herself, and try to guess from Aunt
Bea's response whether it was still welcome. At the same
time she could see how Aunt Bea was settling in at Hampton
Court, and then ring Mother that evening and report.

Royal impulses have built-in safeguards attached, checks
and balances, like the British constitution. Louise had this one
half way through a speech of peculiarly embarrassing self-
importance by the new Director of one of her favourite
charities, Wells for the Sahel; she had been in the Sahel,
looking at its work, only eight months ago, just before her
pregnancy was officially announced. She remembered the

pale grey dust, the flies crawling around famine-huge eyes, the hands too listless to brush them away. Now, as the ghastly man pontificated on and on, she could almost sense the water seeping back down into the aquifers leaving nothing but a slop of mud at the bottom of a hundred expensive holes, as if pulled by the same forces as the dwindling interest of the full-fed financiers round the tables. There was nothing she could do. She had already said her brief bit — she wasn't much of a speaker — her function was to bring the punters in, a barker at the tent of charity. Now this crass egotist was making a mess of the whole effort. She kept her mask of smiling attention fixed but switched her mind off, as far away as possible — snow — the Lowry — the jigsaw, bought that morning en route to the luncheon . . .

Louise was used to the knowledge that at a function like this, and especially with a speaker like this, a good third of the audience would at any given moment be looking not at him but at her. One of the skills Mother had insisted she should acquire, right back in nursery days, was that of opening her handbag, taking out pad and pencil and writing a legible note under the table without moving a muscle that anyone could see. She drooped an arm over the back of her chair with the note between finger and thumb. Constable Evans — just a spare waiter to anyone else at the meal — came to her shoulder and seemed to pick up a napkin from beside the chair. She felt his hand take the note. By the time the speeches were over and Louise had evaded the Director's attempt to monopolise her and done her best to reverse the receding flow of charity by smiles and nods of admiration for two or three big-wigs (double-starred as likely contributors in the unusually good briefing some dogsbody at the charity had sent Joan) the royal impulse had become a Movement Schedule (revised). Evans would have rung Joan at Quercy. Joan would have told Security that HRH would be back an hour late, and why; she would also have rung Aunt Bea; Security would have alerted the people at Hampton Court, and also told the local police that HRH would be passing through; a route would have been agreed, avoiding road-works, and motor-cycle police posted to ease the passage past other bottle-necks — a perk which Louise still felt mildly guilty about, wishing she could have sat out the traffic-jams like any other citizen. Security wouldn't hear of it. They didn't take her crashing though red lights, of course, behind sirening outriders, but they tried to magic her through as if she wasn't there, because the longer she was out on the road, stationary in a jam, especially in an obviously official car after a publicised function from which she could conceivably have been tailed, the more chance there was that somebody might try something. That was what Security said, and though even after Chester Louise couldn't really believe it, she let them have their way. It was seldom worth fighting them. They could make life just as difficult for her as she could for them.

In fact she barely noticed the journey, spending it discussing with Carrie Crupper what if anything to do about the bloody Director. Carrie was the only child of rich, divorced, dotingly demanding parents. By strength of character she had resisted those pressures, insisted on being educated where she chose, mainly in France, and become fluent in three languages. Rather like Piers she seemed to have chosen her own personality, in her case compiling it from opposing elements, street-cred accent, Laura Ashley clothes, cynico-anarchist politics, Filofax-organised days. She'd been making her way up a plush PR firm when Louise had met her. After a couple more meetings, without much hope but because she liked her company, Louise had asked if she'd do a fill-in stint as lady-in-waiting. That had gone well. Carrie had instantly made the job into much more than most people did, and then, unasked, had offered to take it on as one of the regulars for a couple of years. She said it was a good career move, but that might have been one of her jokes.

Ladies-in-waiting have more function that is usually supposed. They have connections — Carrie's were mainly City, a godfather on this set of boards, cronies of her parents on that and that, members of her own circle scrambling up towards t'other. Wells for the Sahel was very much a glossy-brochure and multi-vice-president charity, so Carrie knew some of the people on its council. She could easily call a couple of them about something quite different and mention, as if in passing, that HRH hadn't been very impressed by the Director. That would be quite a big gun to fire at the bastard and Louise was eager to do so, but Carrie gradually whittled her fury away not by saying that the man didn't deserve it but with the old real-world arguments which Louise knew perfectly well — he would have his own power-base: it was still too early in his contract to try and shift him; he'd got good contacts among the tricky Sahel governments; and so on. By the time that the car slid in through the main gate of Hampton Court, Carrie had toned Louise's fury down to manageable disappointment, to be expressed by Joan sending the man only a formal File E letter of thanks. Carrie would ask a few questions, but later. Don't meddle if you can help it, Father always said. (He was a meddler himself, but then he couldn't help it.)

"They never seem to get any further," said Louise, gazing out at the corner of the canvas-covered scaffolding that veiled the state apartments. "How long is it since the fire?"

"Three years? Or four is it? Builders are always the same. Don't matter if it's putting a new loo in a basement flat or rebuilding a palace. They just come and put their mark on a job by knocking a hole in a wall or something. That means no one else can have it and they can go off and finish all the other jobs they'd promised they'd get done the year before last."

"We went round it while it was still swilling with water from the hoses. It was ghastly."

"I just hope Lady Surbiton doesn't go smoking in bed."

"Oh, they don't think the old dear was smoking. She was reading in bed with a candle on her chest."

"Dead mediaeval. I reckon this must be it."

The guard who manned the barrier across the entrance to the private apartments was waiting outside his booth, despite the cold. He swung the pole up with one hand while saluting with the other. The Rolls sighed to a halt. Evans came round and opened the door. Another guard was already saluting by the dark little doorway with the brass plates beside it. I'm going to have a lot less fuss next time I come, thought Louise. The guard ushered them into a murky lobby and rattled the lift-gate open. When he made as if to accompany them up Louise stopped him. The lift, grimy oak with battered brass fittings, doddered up.

"It makes me feel like a wood-worm," said Carrie. "Or a

death watch beetle or something. You know, tunnelling through all this timber."

"Father says that when they were clearing up after the fire they found two residents no one knew existed. They'd just been living here for ever, like spiders in cracks. I think it's just one of Father's stories."

"Surprising Lady Surbiton didn't want to go on living at KP."

"There was a pretty little cottage she could have had, but she was determined to move right out. She can be surprisingly obstinate, under that softness. She said she'd go and live in a hotel till we found her something. It wasn't any problem, actually — there's a lot of apartments empty here. Father's having a battle with Mr Ridley, who can't see why he shouldn't privatise them."

The lift stopped at a dark lobby, the winter light through a small diamond-pane window barely enhanced by that from an iron ceiling-lantern. The door opposite the lift had a brass plate with a name on it, illegible from polishing, like a name on a tombstone. The plate on the door to the left was covered by a card with "Surbiton" lettered onto it in a large, childish hand. A woman was already standing there, leaning on an ebony stick and ringing the bell. She paid no attention at all to the arrival of the lift. The door opened.

"My dear . . . " said Aunt Bea.

She stopped and peered at the woman through her thick-lensed glasses. Her pale face seemed to float disembodied in the gloom, with her mouth opening and closing so that she looked like a fish in an aquarium tank. She pulled herself together and began to apologise in her usual near-whisper, softer than ever now that her increasing deafness had lost her control of it.

"I'm so sorry. I imagined . . . "

"Hello, Aunt Bea," said Louise. "Hordes of visitors."

The strange woman turned at the voice, acknowledging for the first time that there might be someone else in the lobby. Her movement and attitude, as much as the face that now came into view, revealed the cause of Aunt Bea's behaviour, which Louise had taken for characteristic fluster at finding a different caller on her doormat from the one she'd been told to expect. There was more to it than that. In this dim light, and seen with Aunt Bea's vague vision, the woman was Granny.

The moment you looked at her properly, of course, she wasn't. Granny wouldn't have used a stick or worn a neat grey suit with a matching toque. The large brooch in the toque would have been more her line, if the diamonds were real. You couldn't imagine this woman flinging an arm out in one of Granny's whirling gestures, or calling you by absurd and largely invented Russian-sounding endearments, but she stood as straight and carried her head with the same challenge. Her face was from the same mould.

She glanced at Carrie and Louise, apparently without recognition, then turned back to Aunt Bea.

"Lady Surbiton," she said, "I am your neighbour, Mrs Walsh. It is time we made ourselves acquainted. May I come in?"

"Oh, but . . ." began Aunt Bea, but Mrs Walsh was already past her, hobbling with quick, imperious steps along the hallway. Louise stepped forward and kissed Aunt Bea.

"It's all right," she whispered. "Don't send her away. We're hardly staying. If she lives next door you'd better start off on the right foot with her."

Aunt Bea sighed with relief. The idea of her sending anyone anywhere — let alone as formidable an intruder as Mrs Walsh seemed to be — was absurd.

They found Mrs Walsh standing in the middle of Aunt Bea's living-room, looking systematically around. The decor and furniture were pure Aunt Bea, that is to say as dull as human lack of imagination could make them, with a forest-green carpet, cream walls, crackle-parchment lampshades, dozens of slightly out-of-focus snapshots which didn't quite fit their frames, green self-stripe chair-covers with dull gold braid. But the room, with its low ceiling and leaded casement windows and lack of straight edges or square corners, imposed a character of its own, giving a sense of being a cell in this huge old complex, surrounded by scores of similar cells, all of them carrying the imprint of quiet and secretive generations living out their lives there. Beyond the windows, under a dismal December sky, canvas-covered scaffolding

43

veiléd the opposite side of the courtyard where the work was still going on to repair the damage caused by an old lady living just such a life, including a preference for reading in bed with a candle on her chest.

Mrs Walsh seemed now to have recognised who Louise was. She dipped into a centimetre of curtsey but made no effort to leave. Louise, partly to give Aunt Bea as much ammunition as she could for coping with such a neighbour, also out of straight curiosity, stepped forward and shook hands.

"Don't go," she said. "I've only come to give Aunt Bea her Christmas present. Do you know Lady Caroline Crupper?"

Mrs Walsh bowed her head towards Carrie and deliberately as a moving spotlight returned her gaze to Louise, using the convention that one waits for royalty to speak first to maintain herself at the centre of attention. Louise smiled at her and turned to Aunt Bea.

"Can Carrie and I rustle up a cup of tea?" she said. "We've been listening to speeches about deserts."

"Oh, no, my dear. I'm sure I can find everything. I'm still unpacking, bit by teeny bit, but of course I got the tea-pot out first. *So* essential."

"I'll come and help," said Carrie. "Four?"

Mrs Walsh nodded, waited for Louise to sit, and lowered herself into one of Aunt Bea's bungy chairs, where she settled erect, looking regally out of place, like a hawk Louise had seen in a palace in one of the Gulf States on a quilted satin perch.

"Have you lived here long, Mrs Walsh?"

"For fifty years, Your Highness, since my husband retired as Junior Chamberer to His late Majesty."

Did Mrs Walsh have the trace of an accent? Granny's had come and gone as she fancied. Fifty years — Great-grandfather had died in 1938.

"He didn't stay on for my father?" said Louise.

"He was somewhat older than I am, and it seemed convenient to the Palace that the young King should have attendants nearer his own age."

"But you must have known Granny," said Louise. "That'll give you something to talk to Aunt Bea about."

Mrs Walsh for the first time smiled, tight-lipped.

"I fear not," she said. "As Your Highness may be aware, your grandparents' marriage was not welcomed in certain quarters, and communications between the two households were maintained on a merely formal basis. I had in fact met your grandmother once, in Petersburg, when we were both girls, but never in England."

The accent was still indeterminate, but in this slightly longer speech Louise could tell for certain, even before the reference to being a girl in St Petersburg, that Mrs Walsh had not been born English. Her precision of enunciation was like that of some of the German cousins, governess-taught, but the rhythms were slightly different from theirs.

"Are you a Romanov too?" she said. "You look a bit like her."

Again Mrs Walsh smiled her thin smile, expressing not amusement but some error or misconception on Louise's part.

"I am a Belitzin," she said. "It is true that my grandmother was acquainted with the Grand Duke Aleksei Aleksandrovich, whose reputation was such that slander could not be avoided. Had there been any truth in it, which there is not, your grandmother and I would have been second cousins."

Louise nodded. She was long used to the way in which people want to keep their cake of legitimacy and eat it in the shape of a royal connection.

"But family likenesses are extraordinary, aren't they?" she said. "I was looking at my son in his cot the morning Granny died, and suddenly he looked just like her for a bit. I wonder if people with strong characters like Granny are more likely to be taken after. Do you have any children, Mrs Walsh?"

"One, Your Highness."

Not a welcome question, obviously.

"How did you come to England in the first place? During the revolution, I suppose."

Mrs Walsh did not exactly hesitate, but Louise sensed calculation in the brief pause.

"During the revolution, yes. We were fleeing from the Bolsheviks like everyone else. Our major domo bought us places on a train — my mother, my three youngest brothers, two or three servants, all the valuables we could carry. At first we travelled in a little comfort in a proper carriage, though it was very crowded, but then that was commandeered by a general of one of the armies, fleeing like us, and we continued our journey in a cattle truck. Later still our truck was pushed into a siding to wait because an axle had caught fire. The others in the truck crammed themselves into the rest of the train, but my mother decided to wait for another train in the hope that she would know someone in authority aboard and get a carriage again. So we waited. The siding served some mine. There was no town, nothing. Trains went by and did not stop. We finished our food. We waved and screamed at the passing trains. After three days we and the servants dragged timbers onto the track and stopped a train. It was full of soldiers, not Russian, not English — Serbs, I learnt later — going east, defeated, ragged. Some of them climbed out to drag the timbers clear, but when we approached the carriages to plead to come aboard others climbed down and struck at the servants with their rifles and started to drag me and my mother towards the train. We knew at once it was not because they wished to help us. One of my brothers tried to fight them but they cut him down. Then two men came running down the track and began to argue and struggle with the soldiers. One of them had a pistol and shouted at the soldiers in English, so we screamed at him in English, which of course we knew, for help. I was told later that the soldiers were running away from the battle because they had no ammunition left, but the Englishman had bullets for his pistol, so he fired a few shots and forced the soldiers to let us go. By now the track was clear and the soldiers climbed back onto the train, but somebody had found bullets for his rifle and he fired at us and killed one of the Englishmen, so we ran back to our wagon and the train left without us. The Englishman told us the next train would be full of Bolsheviks, so we buried my brother and the dead Englishman and walked away southwards. Fifteen months later we reached England, my husband and I and our daughter. All the others had died on the way. That is how I came to England. I was then seventeen."

Louise felt ambushed. In the nature of her work, visiting

AIDS hospices, refugee camps, famine relief centres, aftermaths of tragedies, she was used to being confronted with stories of everyday but still extraordinary suffering, everyday but still extraordinary endurance. Father used to say that one of the main categories in the royal job-description was specialist social worker. You had to acquire a sort of soft shell which allowed you to feel and express compassion without being overwhelmed. Now, though, she felt momentarily at a loss, having Mrs Walsh's story sprung on her, with its remoteness and horror and illusory romance. It took her an inward blink before the well-worn phrases came to her lips.

"But that must have been terrible! What an adventure! Why doesn't everyone know about it?"

Again that smile.

"There was a time when the world might have known," said Mrs Walsh. "My husband was not a regular soldier. He was an adventurer, an explorer, a passionate anti-Bolshevik. He had attached himself to the Serbian brigade in order to fight for the cause he believed in, and though your War Office had given him some kind of semi-official status in order that he might act as liaison officer with the British contingents, when he returned to England with his health broken after his hardships they refused to accept any responsibility. We sold what was left of my jewels, apart from this, which was given to me by my mother as she died."

She raised a hand to the brooch in her toque. So the diamonds were real, Louise thought. She herself preferred costume jewellery, but there were functions at which she was expected to parade around wearing gew-gaws worth several decent semi-detacheds. The brooch looked in that class.

"We were penniless," said Mrs Walsh. "So we decided to write a book about our adventure. There was a great interest in our war then, and many books published. Nobody cares to remember about it now — it is an embarrassment between the great powers. Be that as it may, we had high hopes of success. But the publishers we had chosen proved weak and incompetent, and when pressure was put on them from certain quarters they made excuses and delayed, and then went bankrupt."

"That's awful!"

"It was, mercifully, the end of our misfortunes. The copies were already printed, and knowing His late Majesty's view on Bolshevism my husband had taken the liberty of sending him one. His Majesty himself, as you may be aware, read very little, but his interest was aroused enough for him to express a wish to meet us, and when he discovered our plight he was gracious enough to offer my husband a post at the Palace, with residence and stipend."

"Yes, I see. Great-grandfather was a funny old thing, but he got it right sometimes. I'd love to read the book. Have you got a copy you could lend me?"

"Sadly, no. The warehouse in which they were stored was bombed in 1942, so we lost every copy."

"And you've never thought of writing it again?"

"No."

"It would make a terrific film."

Mrs Walsh smiled. You could tell she had lived a lot of her life in a formal court, in which only royalty could change the subject so the courtiers had to find ways of signalling that it was time to do so.

"You must have found life a bit dull at the Palace, after everything you'd been through," said Louise.

Mrs Walsh nodded. There was for the first time a sense of some barrier coming down, an acceptance that Louise, unlike most people, was in a position to understand the peculiar boringness of court boredom.

"For myself, no," she said. "After adventures such as we had endured dullness can be very precious. For my husband — he was, as I told you, an adventurer, but . . . "

She fell silent at the movement of the door. Aunt Bea came wheezing in, followed by Carrie with the tea-tray. By the time they had settled and the cups had been poured Mrs Walsh had withdrawn into her hawk-like remoteness. Louise tried to imagine her on her adventure, sixteen — softer-looking then, surely, but with those clear, chilly grey eyes — screaming at passing trains for help, or tramping the immense Russian landscape — they'd gone south, but even there the winters could be icy and they must have got through a winter somehow — the mother dying, the rest of the family too, or lost on the way — and then the love affair with the Englishman who had saved her. Love, really? Looking at her now it was hard to imagine her loving anyone. Seduction? Rape? The mere need to share warmth in sub-zero hutments? Perhaps they'd found some louse-ridden drunken priest, fleeing the Bolsheviks as they were, to marry them. A year of that, the high plateaux, the fierce but uplifting primitiveness of places and people, the endless danger — and then to dwindle into the notoriously stifling ennui of Great-grandfather's court. What a marriage.

"Mrs Walsh has been telling me that she met Granny in St Petersburg when they were both girls," said Louise.

"No!" whispered Aunt Bea.

"And she had astounding adventures escaping from the Communists."

"Dear me. Do you mean to say, Mrs Walsh, that you can actually speak Russian, like HRH?"

"It is my native tongue, Lady Surbiton."

"Well, I must say, that might be very convenient."

"What on earth do you mean, Aunt Bea?"

"Well, you see, my dear, HRH did at one point insist on giving me lessons in Russian, only I was so stupid, and now I have all these letters to sort through. I just thought Mrs Walsh might be interested in helping . . ."

Aunt Bea looked round the other three with the innocent and vulnerable appeal of a child who doesn't expect to understand the adult world, but assumes that someone will come and hold her hand and show her what to do. For the first time it crossed Louise's mind that though it had appeared to everyone that Granny had mercilessly used and abused Aunt Bea — persecuting her with Russian lessons was a typical ploy — the traffic in exploitation might have gone both ways.

"These are letters people wrote to Granny, I suppose."

"Oh, yes, some of them. But do you remember, after the funeral, you brought a man called Alex Romanov to talk to me? There's a whole thick box of copies of letters HRH sent to him. I think that's what they must be. He was talking about them. Carbon copies you know."

"That doesn't sound like Granny at all. Hang on. He did say she'd started using a hard pencil — she'd need that for carbons. They must be absolute hell to read."

49

"Oh, yes, dreadful. Like those scribbles on walls. In Russian, too."

"Honestly, it would be hardly fair on Mrs Walsh . . . wouldn't you do best just to sling the whole lot off to the Palace and ask them to sort it out?"

"Oh, no, my dear. You know what HRH thought of the Palace. And somebody's got to go through them. I've no idea what she's saying, but she could be very, very personal, you know."

Louise glanced at Carrie, who nodded. The signals were a joint mental note, so that in the car Carrie would say "Something about the Dowager's papers?" and Louise would then get out her Filofax and make a physical note to get Joan to telephone Sir Sam . . .

"What did you make of Alex Romanov? — You might have known his mother, Mrs Walsh. Apparently she acted as a sort of gossip-exchange for the whole family."

"We saw very little of the exile community. They centred, of course, round your grandmother, with whom Her late Majesty was barely on speaking terms."

"HRH often said that Queen Mary had swindled her out of millions of pounds worth of jewels," said Aunt Bea.

"I very much doubt whether the jewels in question would have come to Her Royal Highness," said Mrs Walsh. "But it is certainly true that Her late Majesty paid less than a third of their true value for the Dowager Empress's jewellery. We exiles were all in the same case. We sold what we could for what people would pay us. We were fair game."

She spoke calmly, with no bitterness. If anything her reproach was less against Great-grandmama's rapacity than against the Romanovs for making such a fuss about this notorious scandal.

"I liked Count Alex," said Louise. "He's got a lot of charm, hasn't he, Aunt Bea?"

"I suppose so, my dear, but I'm afraid my life has taught me to be just a weeny bit suspicious of charm."

Louise caught Carrie's eye and looked away. The point was that some male gene in the Surbiton line seemed to pass on a unique form of loutishness, as repellent in its attempts to please as in its more usual manifestations of aggression. Aunt

Bea had doted on each generation in turn, down to the present Lord Surbiton, her grandson, now serving a gaol sentence in Japan.

Conversation became the normal vaguely probing exchange you'd expect between new neighbours. Mrs Walsh relaxed her hardness and reserve, if only slightly, and listened to Aunt Bea's sighings and meanderings with patient attention. The subject of offspring naturally arose. Aunt Bea described her grandson's plight with surprisingly deft pre-varications — something legal, but of course the Japanese were so different, there were bound to be misunderstandings, weren't there? Mrs Walsh said only that her daughter lived abroad and hadn't married. You'd have been hard put to find two less well-matched old ladies, Louise thought, but when she rose to leave it was clear that Mrs Walsh intended to stay a bit longer, and just as clear that Aunt Bea wanted her to. They were both lonely, and at least they had the shared experience of court life. That counted for a lot. People outside didn't understand at all.

As on most evenings Louise rang Mother to tell her what she'd been up to. She described the visit to Aunt Bea, and in passing asked Mother to see if Mrs Suttery, the Palace Libra-rian, could find the copy of the book about Mrs Walsh's adventures which had been sent to Great-grandfather. It was probably there somewhere. The Palace had no machinery for actually throwing things away.

Two mornings later, timing her arrival with her usual pre-cision, Joan waddled in to the bedroom with note-book, diaries and post-bag just as Louise was finishing burping Davy after his feed.

"You're looking smugger every day," said Louise.

"Am I? I had one wild night. They were lurching around like Sumo wrestlers. They're going to come out fighting."

Joan pulled out the flap of the escritoire, put the papers on it and took Davy to practise on. She sat down and perched him like a squinting Buddha on the ledge of flesh beneath which her twins, due in three weeks, were housed. Louise started on her make-up.

"We've got thirty-three mins," said Joan. "There's

nothing that couldn't wait till tomorrow, really."

"Let's clear up as much as we can," said Louise. In the mirror over her shoulder she could see Davy and enjoy the way an air of puzzlement would sometimes cross his benign features, probably only caused by a bubble of unrelieved wind but making him look like some indolent gross ruler slowly becoming aware of the revolutionary activities of the twins beneath his throne.

"Nothing new about today," said Joan. "Your speeches and briefings are in the folder. Lady Anne's got copies. You'll have to read the ones for the cement-works before you get to the *spina bifida* place, unless you're going to try and get them read in the helicopter."

"No thanks. Did the Palace OK that bit?"

"They niggled, but I said you were keen. Apparently the local MP is a rabid cost-cutter, but he'll be there and you can wheedle him. They said provided you don't go beyond the script . . ."

"I never do. What's the weather look like?"

"Clear but nippy. There's a bit of fog in Lincolnshire, but they say it'll be gone before you get there. I think that's all about today, but something's just come up about Edinburgh . . ."

"That isn't till . . . when?"

"Thursday week. I'm afraid the Scottish Office have been on to the Palace again saying if Lord Chandler's coming up with you can't he . . ."

"No."

Joan said nothing.

"I'm not even going to ask him," said Louise. "He's coming up to talk to two or three people about his work. They think just because he could fit other things in . . . Oh, God, why can't they tell the bloody people themselves? They know what the answer's going to be. It's just bloody unfair making you ask me and getting us both upset."

"It's all right," said Joan. "Part of the job."

"What on earth am I going to do without you?"

"It'll only be six weeks with luck. I've got a couple of girls coming in today, to look at. There's plenty of time to show them the ropes. It isn't a difficult job, provided you don't get in a fluster."

"Well, *I* couldn't do it."

"I couldn't do yours. I'll bitch at the Palace for you, with pleasure. Now here's something you'll enjoy. Do you remember Chief O'Donovan Kalaki . . . ?"

Janine, already in her out-door clothes, came in to fetch Davy and get him ready for the trip. Louise and Joan worked at the post until the buzzer sounded to tell them that the Daimler was on its way round to the door. As Louise was putting on her gloves Joan said, "Oh, there's a book come from Mrs Suttery. She said you'd asked for it. I've put it in Lady Anne's box, in case you want something to read on the way home."

It smelt of dust-thick shelves. Its pages didn't want to come apart. Its spine crackled. Decades must have passed since anyone had looked at it. No dust-cover. Dark blue linen binding. *Escape from the Reds* by Sirius. Inscribed on the fly-leaf in careful copy-book writing, "With my greatest loyalty and devotion, J.J.Walsh, Major." Published by Danton and Bute in 1922. Illustrations by M.B.W. Frontispiece of an officer, booted and spurred, with a huge holster on his sword-belt and wearing a peculiar fur hat with four up-turned flaps which looked as though they could be pulled down to cover not only his ears but his face and nape as well. He was about thirty-five, already a bit stout, with a fuzzy moustache. He looked in reasonable health, but there was something comic about uniform, figure and pose, as though the costume had been hired for amateur theatricals. Of course he hadn't been an officer in the British Army — the "Major" presumably referred to the temporary rank bestowed on him for his liaison work with the Serbs. Mrs Walsh had described him as an adventurer, but he didn't look the part at all.

About thirty-five in 1922, so perhaps a bit over fifty when Father succeeded in 1938. Father had been only eight, and Granny had already been feuding with the Palace for years, so she would certainly have done her best to create maximum havoc by clearing out all the old courtiers she could, including one dim, semi-invalid figure whose reason for employment in the first place no one could now remember. In fact the Palace had probably fought her off. Granny had lost most of those battles, including the legendary ructions over the Regency, because of her known sympathy for the Nazis. No, surely if she'd been directly responsible for Major Walsh's retirement Mrs Walsh, for all her self-discipline, would have spoken with greater bitterness.

Sadly the book turned out almost impossible to read. Perhaps in 1922, when people knew who General Kornilov was, and what the Bolsheviks had done at Perm, and why the Czechs were the only people who controlled the railway, it might have seemed less bitty and bewildering. Louise, looking for the adventure, skipped rapidly through the first two-thirds of the book, which seemed to be mainly about intrigues between Absolutists and Social Republicans, with rival parliaments sitting in every town and Japanese and French and British and Americans intervening, and counter-orders arriving from London or Paris as soon as any possible compromise had been reached. Then, without warning, in the midst of all this, the adventure seemed to begin.

"Some two hundred miles east of Omsk our train halted for an obstacle on the track. Leaning from my compartment I observed the ruffians from the forward wagons attempting to drag some ladies towards the train. Naturally I intervened, and in the ensuing scuffle my trusty servant, poor Fred Creech, was killed by an unlucky shot from the wagons, no doubt aimed at me. Despite my protestations the train then steamed on without me. Since the next train to pass that way was all too likely to be manned by terrorists I decided to head south, accompanied by the ladies it had been my good fortune to rescue.

"The landscape of the Barabinskay Steppe is an arid plateau, cut by several rivers, sparsely inhabited by nomadic herdsmen. Such agriculture as exists is of a primitive nature, the chief crops being . . . " and so on for page after page, paragraphs that looked as though they had been lifted un-altered from encyclopedias or old *National Geographic Magazines*. The illustrations began here — there had been none in the earlier part of the book — pen-and-ink drawings of "A church burnt by the Bolsheviks", "Our camp by the lake", "Winter quarters", and such. The artist — Mrs Walsh, presumably — seemed not to have been confident of drawing the human figure, but the camp by the lake showed four separate little huts, improvised from branches, whereas the snow scene showed a single shelter, no larger but more solidly constructed, leaning against what looked like the wall of some ruin far older than the burnt church. Had the party huddled into the single hut for warmth? Or had they been fewer already? How had any of them survived? What had they eaten? Ah, Major Walsh had killed a bear, "disposed of the brute with a single well-aimed shot from my revolver". How long would one bear last a family? There was nothing to tell one. The pages between the bear-killing and the point at which "our now sadly depleted party" moved on after the winter were filled with a scornful account of the superstitious nature of the Russian peasant. Surely you didn't get that sort of peasant that far south and east? It was all just padding, noise. There was a message embedded there, a possible marvellous story, but there was no way of reading it through the mess and muddle of the book. It was almost, Louise thought, as though Major Walsh was using every means he could think of not to tell the reader what had happened. The tone, too, was unpleasant, mostly boastful but at times affecting a gentlemanly modesty which rang even less true. There were a lot of references to the virtues of the British officer, and patches of ranting for a policy of invasion through the Himalayan passes and incorporation of all Asian Russia into the British Empire. Louise, still skipping, searching for nuggets of personal adventure, came to a drawing of a dozen dome-shaped tents or portable huts with a few tethered horses. For once the picture was on the same page as the text it illustrated. She read a few lines, found a totally new voice, and continued reading for several pages which described with warm humour life among a group of nomadic Tadzhik herders, people the writer seemed to like and admire, and even to know quite well. The passage ended with the chapter, and the next chapter began with the writer, back in his old voice, now accompanied by "my dear young wife" and building a raft to cross a hitherto unmentioned river.

Deeply disappointed Louise closed the book and drowsed the way to Quercy.

"Danton and Bute, I think. Something like that."

"Never heard of them. You're seriously interested?"

"Yes, I think so."

"I could ask Archie Smith. It's not his period, but he'll know someone."

"You'll have to show him the book. I'll put it for you to take."

"Is your interest more than mere inquisitiveness?"

"Oh, •yes. I am inquisitive, of course. It's such a terrific story. I want to know if it's true. But I was talking to Mother, and she's a bit worried about a tough like Mrs Walsh getting her hooks into Aunt Bea. She thinks we ought to try and find out a bit more about her. And on top of that if Mrs Walsh is going to be reading all the stuff Granny wrote to Alex Romanov about us, people like Sir Sam will want to have her vetted some way or other. She's frightening, but I like her, you know. I want her story to be true. I thought it was but now I'm not sure. The book smells so fake."

"Both could be the case. They arrive in England friendless and live for a while by selling her jewels. He attempts to make some money by writing a book and finds that he isn't up to it."

"He was ill, she said."

"So in desperation he patches something together from other books and magazines and then somehow persuades some hole-and-corner little publisher to take it on."

"I expect so. I still want to know. Mother's going to get the Palace to see if they've got anything about the Walshes in the files."

"All right. I'll get Archie to find someone to have a look at the book. You still haven't told me about your trip. What did Davy make of it?"

"He adored the helicopter. Grinned like an idiot all the time the rotors were going. The ear-muffs wouldn't stay on so we stuffed cotton wool in his ears."

DECEMBER/JANUARY 1987/88

I

"*That you?*"

"*...*"

"*What about Alex Romanov? Any luck?*"

"*...*"

"*We're working on it? You mean you've told the others. What did they say?*"

"*...*"

"*Well, I've got something else you can tell them. It's about the same lot of letters, only copies. This lot are all at Hampton Court. There's an old girl called Lady Surbiton, lives in one of the flats there — the Princess went over to visit her ...*"

2

For once in her life Joan mistimed something. Her labour began a fortnight early, on the afternoon of the day on which she'd started to show Deborah the ropes. The girl-twin was born with a defective heart-valve, and Joan herself suffered from severe internal bleeding because of some complication with the after-birth, and as a result was under intensive care for forty-eight hours. The run-up to Christmas was a fraught period any year, with the staff's nervous energy sparking off into short-circuits caused by the usual personal frets about mums to stay and children to keep busy and travel and catering and so on. Any good cause Louise was involved with was bound to have a carol concert and want her there (the dates would have been in the diary before either Davy or the twins had been thought of) like a goat in the cowshed of charity whose presence was supposed to make the milk flow more freely. Security were always jumpy, too. They'd never tell you if they knew for sure that anyone was planning an attack; it was probably no more than a hunch, based on the knowledge that this was the season when a bomb in Bond Street would cause maximum carnage, so in their eyes other targets, though they mightn't be going anywhere near the West End, were at extra risk as well.

Even without the worry over her illness Joan's dis-appearance from her linch-pin role would have strained the system, and unfortunately Deborah turned out to be one of those people who don't live up to their interviews. Perhaps she found it a problem working for someone six years younger than herself. She was neat and willing and com-petent over anything clear-cut, but no good at nuances. Form letters, for instance, which Joan would automatically have adjusted, were constantly having to be re-typed; little hassles with the Palace which Joan would have coped with herself had to be referred to Louise; and so on. Deborah of course realised she wasn't getting it right, and minded, and became stiff and formal. By the time Louise realised she wasn't going to improve it was too late to look for someone else. Joan was due back in a few weeks, surely? Meanwhile apparent holes in the diary closed, clogged with the extra work, and the strain of the relationship sapped Louise's energy-reserves, so that it was the second week of January before she got a chance to take Davy to show Aunt Bea. Because it was a free afternoon and no movements had been planned or announced for her she drove herself in one of the Rovers with Davy stuffed into his nest-egg beside her and her personal detective, John Dyce, in the back seat. Davy slept most of the way, but opened his eyes in the lift and was already whimpering as she rang the bell. Aunt Bea took a while to answer — Louise had half-expected her, like most lonely old people waiting for a visit, to be almost waiting on the door-mat — so by the time the door opened the whimper had modulated to a Siamese-cat wail.

"Oh, dear," whispered Aunt Bea. "Tummy pains?"

"Just hungry. I'm going to have to feed him. I'll do it in the bedroom if you're squeamish about that sort of thing."

"No, of course . . . Only I've got Maria . . ."

Aunt Bea lowered her voice still further, so that it was inaudible through the wail until Louise craned her ear to the whispering mouth.

". . . meeting her here last time? My upstairs neighbour, Mrs Walsh. I'm *employing* her to help sort HRH's papers. She hasn't a penny of her own, poor dear — she's been living off crusts and scraps from the cafeteria. But she's an absolute boon to me, knowing Russian, so it's a great convenience all round. She works in the spare room so I can ask her to go in there for a while, if you wish."

"Whatever she likes. I don't mind. You go and explain while I take the brat into the bathroom and change him."

As she left Louise saw Aunt Bea hesitate at the living-room door with her lips moving, as if rehearsing for the difficult interview ahead, but when she carried the now dry but squalling Davy into the living-room she found Mrs Walsh still there, standing, with Aunt Bea hovering to one side, a large pale bubble of pure anxiety. Mrs Walsh bobbed into her minimal curtsey and waited, her attitude signalling that Louise herself would have to ask her to leave before she did so. Louise smiled at her, settled into an arm-chair, opened her blouse and hushed the racket.

Aunt Bea sighed with relief.

"Do you know, they wouldn't let us do that," she said. "It was supposed to be unhygienic."

"My child was delivered in a nomad's tent," said Mrs Walsh. "An old hag bit the cord off with her teeth and cauterised it with a live coal."

"And I don't suppose anyone had given you ante-natal classes or anything," said Louise.

"Naturally not. Until the revolution we had been brought up in a glass case, like dolls too precious to play with."

"You must have thought you were dying," said Louise. "Davy hurt like hell for a bit, in spite of the gas-and-air, and you didn't have any of that."

"I had opium. But no, I did not think I was dying. Always, whatever happened, I was certain that I was going to live."

"Maria's incredibly brave," said Aunt Bea. "She's had the most dreadful adventures."

She gazed dimly across the room at Mrs Walsh. Though perfectly clean and kempt she reminded Louise of an Old English Sheepdog gazing out from under its shag of eyebrows, a poor old bitch which had lost her mistress and then, after a period of bewildered grief, had transferred her devotion to a new owner. Mrs Walsh too appeared happy with the relationship, and seemed to have been encouraging it by regaling Aunt Bea with extracts from her escape. It was certainly good to see Aunt Bea up from the pit of mourning, but Louise didn't feel fully happy with the change — a doormat may perhaps only find fulfilment in having shoes wiped on it, but when it's a lovable old thing like Aunt Bea you can't help wishing it a year or two of some other kind of existence before it goes to the bonfire.

"You seem to have made yourself pretty snug," said Louise.

Sighingly Aunt Bea agreed. Of course it was rather a long way from the shops, but she'd got her little car; and last week the lift had failed for three whole days; and the workmen over on the other side of the courtyard did make a noise with their wirelesses on full blast in the early morning . . . she glanced every now and then at Mrs Walsh, as if anxious that she might be saying something not permitted. Mrs Walsh, herself spoke very little, but by the nature of her silences managed to occupy her third part of the conversation. Since a secondary motive for the visit had been to try and find out a bit more about her, and whether any urgent steps needed to be taken to stop her having the run of Granny's papers, in the end Louise addressed her directly.

"I found a copy of your husband's book," she said. "He'd presented one to Great-grandfather, and it was still in the Library."

Mrs Walsh raised her eyebrows and sat waiting, expressionless.

"We weren't taught that bit of history," said Louise. "I got a bit lost in the first part — all those generals and parties, and not knowing whose side anyone is on. I wish there'd been a bit more about your actual adventure, things like your baby being born in a tent, you know."

"My husband was not present. When a baby was born,

all the men left camp."

"Still . . ."

Louise stopped. As on her last visit, but even more strongly, Mrs Walsh had managed to signal that she would prefer the subject changed. Louise felt obstinate.

"That must have been when you were among the Tadzhiks," she said. "Have I pronounced that right? You did a picture. Funny round tents like bowler hats without a brim, and horses."

"The tents are called *yurts*. They are made of mats on a frame. Your Highness, forgive me — this book. I possess no copy at all. I have not seen one for forty years. I barely remember what is in it and what is not — it was my husband's work, not mine. I should at least like to hold it in my hands again."

"Yes, of course. Next time I come. I don't know if I can actually give it to you — I'll have to find out. You remember what that sort of thing's like at the Palace?"

"Of course."

"Were the pictures ones you'd done on the journey, or did you do them from memory after?"

"I carried my sketch-pad with me. I used it to remind myself of the time when I was a doll in a glass case. My husband simply took the drawings for his book."

His book, now. Hadn't it been *we* before who decided to write it, *our* publisher who messed things up?

"Oh, but it's all so fascinating!" said Aunt Bea. "Such dreadful times! And so brave! How I wish HRH could have been here to talk to you!"

That would have been a meeting of Titanesses, perhaps a battle for poor Aunt Bea's soul. Louise wasn't at all sure that Granny would have got the best of it.

"You must tell the Princess about your husband pretending to be ill and running away with all the horses," said Aunt Bea. "And crossing the river!"

"There's a bit about crossing the river in the book," said Louise, "but . . ."

She was interrupted by an alteration in the rhythm of Davy's sucks. He was already almost as obsessively regular in his bodily functions as his grandfather, and if Louise had been an ordinary citizen she would have been tempted to pot him, as she herself had been potted pretty well from birth. The trouble was, some woman's-mag hack would be sure to find out, and next thing a whole generation of Britons would find themselves being pot-trained straight from the womb, with unknowable effects on the national psyche. But at least his Old-Faithful-like predictability meant that she could clean him up pretty well on the instant, with fewer leakages and changes of clothing than most mums had to cope with, so now she carried him off into the bathroom and sorted him out. When she brought him back into the living-room she was at once aware that Aunt Bea was in the grip of a fresh bout of anxiety. Louise smiled, exuding motherly calm.

"All safe and sound," she said.

"I'm so glad. You are marvellous, doing it all yourself. But, well, um, we've heard from Dr Romanov, you know. He wants to come and take HRH's papers away. I can't think what to do. I don't like to trouble HM, but really . . ."

"Alex is Granny's literary executor, you see. She put it in her will."

"Yes, I know, dear, but . . ." wavered Aunt Bea.

Mrs Walsh rescued her decisively.

"We are by no means ready to hand the papers over to anyone. It will be several more weeks before we have been through everything. The Dowager's hand is exceedingly difficult to read, especially in the carbon copies. I am having to use a reading-glass much of the time. And in the meanwhile Beatrice should certainly have advice on the legal aspect of her responsibilities."

"You'd better ring Sir Savile's office," said Louise. "I should think Jane Gordon-Byng is the person to talk to — she's a proper lawyer. She'll know what you're on about — I told Mother after my last visit that you'd got all Granny's papers, and she'll have passed it on. They haven't been in touch with you?"

Knowing the answer Louise felt a flicker of shiftiness about the question. Provided Mrs Walsh could be trusted the Palace were perfectly happy for Aunt Bea to be as obstinately long as she wished before handing any papers over to an outsider. It was only intense and automatic secretiveness (which Louise

62

couldn't help sharing to some extent) which had made them suggest that Louise should deal with the matter on a casual footing, as though Granny's papers were only of minor interest to anyone. For Aunt Bea to ring the Palace herself would now allow them to deal with her directly, without their having alerted her by making the first move themselves.

"I don't think you need worry too much about Dr Romanov," said Louise. "As a matter of fact I'm having supper with him this evening and I'll try and do a bit of gentle probing. I haven't seen him since the funeral, but Piers has talked to him a couple of times about their work. He says he seems a reasonable sort of person. I suppose he might want his own letters back, if Granny bothered to keep them."

"I have found a number of letters from Count Aleksei," said Mrs Walsh. "They seem of very little interest at a super-ficial reading. Third-hand tittle-tattle, and misinformed."

"He's rather amusing to meet," said Louise.

"They may well be amusing, to people who are amused by that sort of thing. The Dowager Princess's letters to him are of the same order. I find it hard to imagine why she troubled to keep copies."

Louise smiled, doing her best to encourage the dismissive attitude. It didn't sound as if Mrs Walsh was about to start telephoning The *Daily Mail* with translated titbits.

"Oh, you could never tell why HRH chose to do any-thing," said Aunt Bea. "I keep thinking, suppose the poor Prince hadn't drowned like that . . . People say she didn't really love him, but she did, she did. When she thought no one was listening she used to talk to him still, you know. Teasing him. Little bits of baby-talk. Of course I always pretended I hadn't heard."

"They had been married how long?" said Mrs Walsh.

"Just over ten years, wasn't it, Aunt Bea?"

"That is a very good time to lose your husband," said Mrs Walsh, with a banal finality, as if laying down the law on the proper season for the spraying of peach-trees. Louise was saved from having to answer by the beep of the pager from her handbag.

"Bother," she said. "Somebody's after me. Do you mind, Aunt Bea?"

63

She rose with Davy still leeched to her breast and juggled one-handed in her bag to check the number of the Rover car-phone.

"Lucy Ford," she said. She always felt a bit of a fool using the security code when anyone was listening, but John Dyce would have to report her if she didn't.

"There's an alert, ma'am."

"A real one?"

"Sounds like it."

"You mean something's happened?"

Davy gave a fretful snort as the chill of tension cut off his milk supply. Bert and Soppy were due in Belfast tomorrow, on a post-Christmas cheer-the-troops whirl. It was secret, of course, but you could never be sure.

"Not that I know, ma'am. They just said to check your timing."

"We'll have a cup of tea and go. Half an hour?"

"I'll tell them."

"Perhaps you'd better look out a different route home."

"I'm doing that. Not to worry, ma'am."

Louise put the handset down and turned, smiling.

"Sorry about that," she said. "It wasn't anything."

Still, it was more than a minute before Davy could suck satisfactorily again. This sort of thing happened about once a week, Louise thought, but Security didn't usually tell you about it unless you were alone and unwatched.

"Let me get the tea ready, Beatrice," said Mrs Walsh, rising. "You will need to come and carry the tray. I will call you when it is ready."

She left the room, using her stick to lean on more heavily than on Louise's last visit. Aunt Bea gazed after her till the door closed.

"Isn't she wonderful?" she whispered. "Such a good head, and so sure of herself. She tells me I ought to assert myself more."

"The girl who's minding me while Joan's having the twins goes to self-assertion classes."

"Classes? With desks and blackboards?"

"I think they act little plays asserting at each other. She says it helps. Don't worry, Aunt Bea — everyone likes you as you are. Why didn't Mrs Walsh want us to go on talking about her adventure?"

Aunt Bea's doughy pallor was incapable of blushing, but everything else proclaimed her embarrassment.

"Oh . . . oh . . . well, you see, my dear, you're so young."

"Not in front of the children?"

"It's all right for us old things who've knocked about a bit . . ."

Aunt Bea was no fool. She knew she was talking nonsense. She'd seen videos of Louise at bedsides in the harrowing hospitals of refugee camps, babies born after accouchements as primitive as the one Mrs Walsh had been describing with such relish. It was a rotten fib, and she knew it, but Louise couldn't hound the poor old thing any further, so she let Davy finish his feed and then handed him over to Aunt Bea to be burped while she went into the kitchen to fetch the tray.

During tea Mrs Walsh talked very forthcomingly about her life in St Petersburg before the First World War. The family had lived close to the Catherine Embankment, and strong among her childhood memories was the daily walk, with perambulators and nursemaids, past the spot at which Tsar Alexander had been assassinated thirty years earlier. One of the nurses, she said, used to describe the attack, always in the same words, ritualised like a fairy-tale, the racing carriage, the explosion, the Tsar climbing down to inspect the damage, and then the second explosion and the screams, and the smoke clearing away to show the Tsar and his assassin lying almost side by side, bleeding their lives out into the snow. Louise took Davy from Aunt Bea and sat nodding and oohing while she ran her fingers up the elastic little back, easing the knots of wind in the tubing. Of course, she realised, Mrs Walsh was talking so freely in order not to have to answer questions about her later adventure. She couldn't know how close the Chester bomb had come to doing the same thing to Mother and Father — that had been largely hushed up, and most of the trial had been *in camera*. All the same, it was pretty tactless. Deliberately? Probably not. With a personality as powerful as Mrs Walsh's, the most trivial phrase or gesture tended to seem deliberate.

It was cold when Louise came out into the open, and dark

under the cloud-layer, though it was still well before dusk. She slid the nest-egg across onto the passenger-seat, expecting John to be ready at the other door to fasten the seat-belt round it, but he was standing well back from the car, one hand in his jacket pocket, glancing left and right along the worn old façade with its nooks and crannies and buttresses. He didn't climb in until she had the engine started.

"Looks as if it might snow," she said.

"Feels that way, ma'am."

But not blood, she thought. No one's blood.

Piers rang before she'd been home five minutes.

"Ah, there you are," he said. "All all right?"

"Yes, why?"

"Oh, well, one of your minders rang to check my movements, but he wouldn't tell me anything. Just said not to worry, which was counter-productive. What happened?"

"Probably nothing. They didn't tell me either. Anyway they haven't asked us to cancel supper."

"That's what I'm ringing about. I'm afraid Adrian's got flu. Tracy says she's had it and isn't infectious but do we still want her? I said yes."

"Good. While I've got you — you remember that book, the one about Mrs Walsh and her husband escaping from the Bolsheviks . . ."

"Talking about it only this morning. Archie gave it to a chap called Harrison — I don't know him — who passed it on to one of his students. The student has apparently read it. Harrison rang to ask if we wanted a written report, or what."

"Oh, no — I just want to talk to him — the student, I mean. I say, you couldn't get hold of him for this evening? He could fill in for Adrian. If he's free, I mean."

"You don't want me to issue a royal command?"

"No, of course not. See you later."

She rang off, irritated. He shouldn't have asked, though he'd meant it as a joke. This was supposed to be one of her ordinary-person evenings, but he'd reminded her that there weren't many real ordinary people who wouldn't have cancelled other engagements, however pressing, if like this unnamed student they'd been asked at the last minute to join her.

Piers had kept his ramshackle little flat near the university partly because he sometimes needed it but also because Louise could then use it to act bits of that fantasy life in which she was just Mrs Chandler, and nothing much else. In the early days of their marriage she'd tried to go the whole hog, doing all the work herself. She was a barely adequate cook, but that wasn't the main problem. Shopping, for instance, only emphasised the unreality of the fantasy. Other shoppers were mostly unintrusive, but there was something about dithering in front of a meat display with a dozen people watching out of the corner of their eyes to see what she bought that made her panic and choose wrong. It was absurd. Most of her job consisted in being stared at, but that didn't help. She'd read that professional strippers were often as prudish as anyone else off-stage. All Louise was, she sometimes thought, was a stripper who didn't undress. Anyway, Chester happened, and Security put their foot down about popping in to Sainsbury's and it was a relief.

Security would have liked to stop the parties in Piers's flat and let Louise have her guests over to Quercy, but as Father said you had a sort of duty to the Family as a whole to insist on your own small freedoms, or you'd all finish up living in separate bunkers and being brought out on state occasions to be whisked through the streets in bomb-proof carriages like the poor old Tsar, and look how much good that had done him. So nowadays Mrs Newton was driven over from Quercy in the afternoon to get everything ready, and all Louise needed to do was remember to turn the cooker off before she dished up.

The student's name turned out to be Don Brown. He was about twenty-five, tubby and crop-haired, with a strongly American look but with an equally strong Scots accent. He shook hands but didn't smile. Piers had brought him along, and Tracy and Isabelle arrived less than a minute later, so Louise merely said hello and took Tracy off to the kitchen, ostensibly to help her check that the cooking was on course but really to catch up in private on the latest episode of

67

Tracy's medical cliff-hanger. Tracy was as healthy as anyone else, on average, but seemed to have the psychic ability to cause any doctor who looked at her to produce a wrong and usually alarming diagnosis, so that by her own account (foul-mouthed and in a dispassionate, flat Midland voice) she had spent a third of her life fighting her way out of operating theatres just in time to save kidney or spleen, or with Adrian desperately trying to persuade the psychiatric nurses who'd turned up on the doorstep that the alarming symptoms she'd been displaying two days ago had ceased since she'd stopped taking the last wrong lot of pills she'd been prescribed. She managed to regard these episodes as being both a serious outrage and pure farce. The current series, obscene even by Tracy's standards, concerned the latest attempts to achieve a long-wanted pregnancy. It was sad, because it didn't look as if anything was going to happen — but by the time they went back into the living-room Louise had barely managed to control her laughter and now had hiccups.

Alex must have just arrived. Piers was watching with benign mild malice to see how he took Isabelle's treatment of any new man she met, which consisted of batting cartoon-size eyelashes at him and at the same time rattling through a questionnaire on such things as his opinion of the novels of Walter Scott, post-modernist hypermarkets, the landscape of Umbria, heroic tapestry and Scriabin. Alex was beaming, clearly loving the game and batting back counter-questions. Mr Brown, who had no doubt gone through the same culture-mill but with less enjoyment, was watching. He almost jumped round as Louise approached him. She could feel his nerves, poor man. Some people reacted like that, and there wasn't much you could do about it — not just students and other innocents but people you'd have thought knew how to cope, directors of large firms, admirals, bishops even. You could feel them vibrate as if responding to some kind of mystic ray you were beaming out at them. Usually a few minutes of chat would calm them, but sometimes they went on twanging all the time you were with them, and it became difficult not to twang in harmony. Mr Brown, Louise guessed, had the added problem of having believed he didn't bother himself much about royalty, either way, and now finding that this wasn't true.

"Don't worry about Isabelle," she whispered. "She won't keep it up. It's just her way of showing she isn't just a brilliant boffin. Drat. If this goes on I'm going to have to hold my breath. How've you been getting on with my book?"

"Um . . . well . . . um . . . ma'am . . ."

"Is it really only a lot of stuff lifted from other books? I mean that's what it reads like, isn't it?"

Mr Brown looked relieved. The vibrations lessened. No doubt the hiccups helped.

"I haven't traced it all yet, of course, er, ma'am . . ."

"You just say it once and then forget about it. But you've found bits like that?"

"*With the Diehards in Siberia* by Colonel John Ward. Sirius has copied extensively from that throughout the opening chapters. Occasionally he inserts paragraphs from other sources — more than one, I think — but I haven't traced them yet."

"That's what I thought. Really, it's the second half I'm interested in, after he leaves the train. I want to know if any of it's true. I'll tell you what happened. I met an old lady who told me this marvellous story about escaping from Russia during the revolution. It was the most romantic thing I'd ever heard. Of course I wanted to know more and when she said her husband had written a book about it I asked if I could borrow a copy, but she said they'd all been destroyed in the blitz. Then I found this one in the Palace Library — the husband had sent it to my great-grandfather and they never throw anything away — but I was terribly disappointed when I read it. There's hardly anything about the adventure at all, is there? I'm not just being inquisitive, by the way. I've got to know whether the old lady I was talking about is above board, if you see what I mean."

"I can find no trace of the book having been published."

"That's right. She says pressures were put on the publishers from certain quarters. I don't know what that means."

"By Colonel Ward's publishers, presumably — Cassells, I think. The book would have been sent to the same reviewers, and some of them would have got in touch with Cassells.

Danton and Bute wouldn't have had a leg to stand on. They'd have been forced to withdraw the book before publication, for breach of copyright. Mr Sirius must have been dead naive."

"He was an adventurer, she says. He might have been a sort of gentleman con-man, who'd somehow got involved in that bit of war. He seems to have conned my great-grandfather, but that wasn't difficult. She says Danton and Bute went bankrupt."

"Having to withdraw the book could have bust them. Do you know . . . Sorry . . . They told me I wasn't supposed to ask questions."

The next hiccup came in the middle of Louise's laugh, and hurt. Before she'd recovered the kitchen buzzer sounded.

"We'll have to leave it for the moment," she said. "But listen. I've got a problem. It's a bit embarrassing, but I only thought about it on the way over. Alex Romanov will be on my other side, and for reasons I can't tell you I don't want to get him involved in this book. It's nothing sinister, just awkward. You might find him interesting in other ways, though. He knows a lot of old exile gossip."

Mr Brown nodded, already, despite himself, a loyal servant of the Crown. Louise scuttled off to dish up, holding her breath as she did so, but her hiccups resisted the treatment. The subject came up again before she had taken her second spoonful of melon.

"How's life been treating you?" she asked Alex.

"Benevolently at the moment, ma'am. The only cloud in my sky is that I am having unexpected difficulties with dear Lady Surbiton. For reasons known only to herself she has taken all the Grand Duchess's papers with her to Hampton Court, and now appears to have hired a dragon to protect her hoard. A dragon fluent in Russian, what's more."

"Mrs Walsh. Her upstairs neighbour. She's helping Aunt Bea sort Granny's papers."

"She didn't vouchsafe even that much on the telephone. All she will say is that Lady Surbiton isn't yet ready to see me. If I have the good fortune to be answered by Lady Surbiton herself she hands me over at once to the dragon. I suppose I should be grateful that they are doing the tedious part of a literary executor's job for me, but I would prefer to undertake it myself. Do you think there is any danger of their deciding to destroy anything?"

"Oh, I hope not. I mean, I know Aunt Bea's worried about the sort of things Granny probably said about people, but . . . Tell you what — I'll ring the Palace tomorrow and get them to tell her not to."

"And this Mrs Walsh is to be trusted, you think? In other ways?"

"We're trying to find out. She's got a hold on Aunt Bea because she looks a bit like Granny. The first time I met her I asked if she was a Romanov too."

"Is she?"

"She said no, but she as good as told me her grandmother had been friendly with a Grand Duke Aleksei who had a bit of a reputation."

"Aleksandrovich, presumably."

"That's right."

"Fast women and slow ships," said Mr Brown, getting his oar in rather too firmly from Louise's other side. Alex gave him a blink of encouraging surprise.

"Mr Brown's doing research in that period," said Louise.

"Later — some of the émigré pamphleteers," said Mr Brown. "But I have to know the antecedents. The Grand Duke had a penchant for ballet-dancers, didn't he?"

"Oh, Mrs Walsh is grander than that," said Louise. "Her family name's Belitzin."

"Belitzin?" said Alex. "I don't know of any Belitzins. Very grand, you say? It wasn't, for instance, Belayev?"

"No, Belitzin. A lot of my job's getting names right."

Alex looked across at Mr Brown, who shrugged ignorance.

"I know a bit about the Belayevs, of course," he said. "There were four of them still raising hell in Paris in my period, challenging everyone to duels and so on. One of them ran an Absolutist sheet for a few months, and two of the others put on counter-agitprop melodramas — there was one with a climax in the Ekaterinburg cellar which caused a riot when a lot of leftists packed the audience and broke the theatre up."

"Yes, I remember my mother talking about it," said Alex.

"The Belayevs were always interested in the theatre — they'd a family tradition of maintaining their own troupe of actors — or rather they employed servants who could also act. They insisted on their learning English, too, so that they could perform Shakespeare in the original language. Were there any daughters in that generation? I don't think so — just seven wild boys. Of course it could have been another branch of the family, but really, if a Countess Belayev had had a liaison with the Grand Duke Aleksei and produced a genuine Romanov by-blow my mother would certainly have told me. She took a veritably scholarly interest in such ramifications."

"She isn't a spitting image of Granny," said Louise. "She just has that look."

"And she is now living at Hampton Court in a grace and favour apartment?" said Alex.

Louise nodded. She was aware of having told him more about Mrs Walsh than she'd meant to. His charm made it hard not to assume that he was already on your side in any difficulty or dispute. She looked for a way of half-changing the subject.

"What's her Russian like?" she said. "Sorry, they'll go away in a minute — Tracy was making me laugh in the kitchen. I mean, I don't even know if Russian's like English used to be in that generation, so you could tell from the way people spoke whether they were what my Uncle Ted would call pukka."

"Oh, absolutely pukka. Very grand, very old-fashioned . . . the thing is, ma'am, I need to get past this dragon, to pacify or conquer it somehow. I must get Lady Surbiton to understand that she has no right to keep the papers. She should never have had them in the first place. I've taken legal advice, and it would be possible to insist — to take Lady Surbiton to court, if necessary . . ."

He shrugged and smiled, waiting for Louise to finish holding her breath. With one part of her mind she went on counting, while with another she wondered whether the naturalness of the gesture held any kind of threat. Impossible, it had said. Think of the fuss, the hordes of hacks, the offers from magazines and publishers . . . You'd much better help me make Aunt Bea see reason.

"Whoo," she said. "Let's hope that's done it. Have you been in touch with the Palace? Jane Gordon-Byng's the person to talk to, I should think."

"I have an appointment to meet Mrs Gordon-Byng next week, at which I hope to make some progress. She has been entirely friendly and sympathetic on the telephone, only nothing seems to happen, and I'm beginning to think that is how the Palace would prefer things to remain. I am not prepared to accept that, and if they won't help me I will have to do what I can on my own. Our interests with regard to Mrs Walsh, at least, are the same. We both need to know a bit more about her."

"You mustn't worry about the Palace. They're always like that. You have to push and push to get them to move at all. But honestly I don't really understand why you're so anxious about it. I mean, did Granny write anything serious, apart from that coffee-table book about harps — and I'd be surprised if that was all her own work, anything like?"

"That's why I need to look at the complete papers. I really must for my own sake get this job cleared up. In some of the letters she sent me she refers to memoirs she's writing, mostly about her childhood in Russia."

"Do you think she'd have stuck to it?"

"How can I tell, until I've seen the papers? It may be publishable fragments. On the other hand it may be mere wishful thinking. Then there is the question of a biography. She certainly assumed there would be one and suggested possible authors. Any biographer would need the use of her papers, and my assent as literary executor. How could I give that without having seen them? Then there are the letters themselves, though in view of their contents I imagine there would be a certain resistance from the Palace to their publication in full . . . "

"Damn," said Louise. "It hasn't worked. I'm going to have to try something else."

Nothing in fact worked. The hiccups persisted all evening. After supper Louise managed to permute her guests around to her satisfaction. The party broke up soon after midnight.

"I've still got them."

"So I notice. Pope Pius had them for three years, I seem to remember. What did Davy make of them?"

"Didn't approve at all. Couldn't make out whether it was him or me."

"How did you get on with Alex?"

"Like a house on fire, one way. He's very easy to talk to. I was pretty well above board, apart from not telling him about Mrs Walsh's book. I told him the Palace would want to see what was in the letters, because Granny was bound to have libelled half the people she mentions. He says that she left instructions for him attached to her will. She wants everything published, and the profits to go to some kind of music charity. He feels he's got to try and get something off the ground. He was just thinking about a book — he didn't even mention the hacks."

"I don't believe he can be that naif."

"Nor do I."

"Anyway, any publisher would want to recoup by serialisation — in the *Sunday Telegraph*, most likely."

"He says he's got his copies in a bank now. He went a bit out of his way to tell me."

"That certainly doesn't sound naif."

"I'd love to see Sir Sam sneaking around in a mask and a striped jersey with a sack labelled 'Swag'."

"Do you really think they'd go that far?"

"Faking a burglary? I don't know. You just can't tell when Security get the bit between their teeth. That's why I'm going to see to it that if there's any negotiating to do with Aunt Bea it's either Mother or me who does it."

"What about Mr Brown?"

"I liked him. I wish it was easier to meet his sort more often, without fuss. It was nice having a reason for him to be there, so he didn't just feel on parade. He agrees with me the book's a fake, lifted from other books. He's found the main one for the first part. He couldn't help much about the adventure. I'd asked him not to talk about the book in front of Alex, because I didn't think it was fair to give Alex that kind of hold, but it turned out he was much more interested in the exile period so he and Alex spent most of their time sorting that out."

"I saw you'd swapped chairs."

"I'm not used to being talked across."

"Do you good."

"They didn't actually, but I could see it would make life easier, and anyway I thought it was about time you paid a bit of attention to Tracy. You have Isabelle to yourself all day long."

"A totally different Isabelle, whom I rather prefer, if you wish to know."

"Come off it."

"But I have to admit I find Tracy slightly heavy going."

"Do you really? I think she's terrific. You know she and Adrian were childhood sweethearts? It was ages before she realised he wasn't going to carry on at his dad's greengrocery. She swears she only got acquainted with him in the first place because she liked bruised bananas. I wish she could have some children. You know, most of your colleagues' wives can't help behaving as if they were almost-dons themselves, but Tracy says the hell with it. When people sort of hint that actually I don't have much idea what ordinary people are like, I think about Tracy. She's the real thing."

"Everybody is in one sense genuine and in another sense fake. We all have to invent our own persona as a carapace for our inner incoherence. What you call genuineness in Tracy's case simply means that her self-invention was largely unconscious, whereas in a case like Alex's, or even more in mine, it is much more deliberate and willed."

"Mrs Walsh too."

"You seem, if I may say so, to be a little Walsh-obsessed at the moment."

"You haven't met her. She's really something. A natural force. I've come to the conclusion that what's happening there is that Mrs Walsh likes dominating Aunt Bea and Aunt Bea likes being dominated, but they can't just start in on a relationship like that as if they were the only people in the world. They've got to have an excuse, something to be dominant and dominated about. Granny's papers are perfect.

75

And of course Aunt Bea is paying Mrs Walsh to help her and Mrs Walsh hasn't got a bean, despite swanning around with a forty-carat diamond in her hat, so she's got a good straight ordinary motive for spinning the work out as long as she can by fighting us and Alex off. The question is, if she's that keen on the money, mightn't she realise what she could make by slipping the odd titbit to the hacks? If I had to bet on it I'd say no."

"Not realise? Or not slip?"

"Both, I think. Especially if she's already pretty jumpy — I don't know what about, but she is. What do you think?"

"I would be inclined to risk it, though for different motives. You don't want to do anything that might bring Security in on the act. Alex, by the way, tells me that he's under the impression that he's been vetted in some way."

"I suppose so."

"You approve?"

"No. Yes. No. I don't know. It's just something people have to put up with if they're going to have us there at all. Like sending the sniffer dogs in to a kids' home before I go and visit them. If Alex is going to have direct dealings with us Sir Sam is bound to have told Security, and they're bound to have run an eye over him. It's what they're there for. I mean, suppose his girl-friend's a member of the Red Brigade . . . or boy-friend, I suppose . . . what d'you think?"

"Why don't you ask Security?"

"Darling, it can't be helped. It's one of the things you married."

"Of course."

"All right. Be like that . . . I've thought of a cure for hiccups."

"Hm?"

"Hm?"

FEBRUARY 1988

I

"*That you?*"

"*...*"

"*Listen, you can forget about Alex Romanov — he's gone and put all his lot of letters in a bank. It shows they're important, though, doesn't it, him doing something like that?*"

"*...?*"

"*Lady Surbiton? There's two of them in it, matter of fact — the other's called Mrs Walsh, and there's something fishy about her — they don't know what. Anyway, the Princess has been over to see them again — she's handling it all herself — that's another thing, shows how they want to keep it all hushed up. So you see . . .*"

2

It was sheer bad luck, the sort of thing that happens when you're down already, just one hack in the wrong place — not even a royal-watcher either.

Apparently he was snuffling round on the trail of a bullion-robber who was rumoured to be holed up in Argentina. He had heard vague talk of comings and goings at a little provincial airport and had gone along to question the ground staff. His entry was barred, without explanation, so naturally he assumed he was onto something. After a grumble or two he drove away out of sight, parked his car and made his way back on foot to the perimeter fence just in time to see the private jet come in. He had his telephoto camera ready and got a very good picture in the two or three seconds when Soppy had taken her sunglasses off to kiss the wife of the billionaire polo-crony to whom the jet belonged. Even at that distance, even wearing a wig, she was unmistakable.

Louise woke up to the news. The BBC of course were doing their best to play it down, tuck it away, treat it as only a rumour, waffle on about the Princess's private visit to Florida, but you could tell from the tone of voice that they knew it was true, and serious. They just didn't wish to be seen in the front row of vultures prodding their beaks into the kill.

"Oh, God!" she said.

"What's up?" said Piers.

He had an extraordinary ability not to hear information which didn't interest him, as though he could physically stuff his ears with rolled-up pellets of pure thought. Louise explained.

"It might even be my fault," she said. "I did say something to Bertie about smuggling her out to Argentina in a false nose. Anyway, nobody's going to believe we didn't all know. Oh, God!"

"Aren't you over-reacting?"

"No. I'm worried stiff for Bert and Soppy. It's pretty well certain to come out that they've been having a rocky patch, and with Soppy being hounded night and day that can only get worse. There's a real chance she'll go round the bend. Then there's us. If the hacks decide Father didn't know what was up that'll make it worse for Soppy, splits in the family — can't you just see it? And if they think he did it'll be a constitutional crisis — it'll be one anyway. *And* he's got Mrs T. to cope with. She'll be raging."

"Enraging her is a popular move."

"Be serious, darling. You realise you're going to have to tell your switchboard to tell everyone you're in a meeting or something. And . . . "

The telephone rang.

"Lulu?"

"I've just heard the news."

"You didn't know before?"

"I thought she was going to Florida. Poor Soppy."

"Poor Soppy. You realise what a bloody awful potmess she's landed us in?"

"Yes, but . . . she's right at the end of her tether, Father. I talked to her about it at Granny's funeral. Even then . . . Did Bert know?"

"Not answering his private line. Not available on his switchboard. What do you mean, end of her tether?"

"Bert talked to me too. He was pretty bothered. I told Mother."

"Oh yes, I remember. All marriages go through phases. Anyway, it's a totally inadequate excuse. By God, if Bert put her up to it . . ."

An answering scream of fury burst from the baby-alarm, as though it had suddenly been switched on with Davy already in full cry. Louise pressed the S button.

"Go and ask Janine to pick him up, darling," she said and pressed the S again.

"Are you there, Lulu?"

"Sorry, your grandson had started to yell too. I've got the generations bawling at me from both sides. Hold it again . . ."

Janine was already at the door, before Piers had reached it. She had a purple-faced Davy in her arms.

"Not in here," said Louise. "Try and keep him quiet for five mins. Sorry, Father. No, listen. Shut up and listen. You've got it wrong. This is a mess, like you say, and I wish to God it hadn't happened, but that's not the important thing about it. The most important thing is we've got to try and help Soppy. And Bert. It *isn't* just a phase they've been having. They're both desperately unhappy and Soppy's on the edge of some kind of breakdown. That's what really matters. So what you've got to do is get onto Bert somehow or other and instead of yelling at him like a mad major *ask* him — don't get Mother to do it, ask him yourself . . ."

"Ask him what, for God's sake?"

"What we can do to help. Nothing about whether he knew, or why she's bolted, or any of that. Do you understand?"

"She's right, Vick."

"Bloody line's bugged."

"Hello, Mother. Don't you think . . ."

"One moment, Lulu. Vick, I have Bert on my line. Will you talk to him?"

79

"Will I bloody not! I've got the PM coming at ten!"

"Now listen, Father . . ."

"All right, all right, I heard what you said. Call you later, Lulu."

The telephone didn't go dead. Louise could hear Mother's cool lilt as she talked to Bert on the other line, the thump of a door, a pause, and then Father's voice, level, calm and conciliatory. As she put the handset down it struck her that she had never talked to him like that before. She had argued with him, often, and had had soul-wrenching rows during her struggle to be allowed to marry Piers, but she'd never before shut him up in the middle of one of his rages and then told him how *he* should do things.

"May I go and get dressed?" said Piers.

"I'll be down as soon as I've fed the brat. Will you be off before that?"

"I'm behind time already."

"All right. Give us a kiss. Don't forget to tell the switchboard you're in meetings all day."

"You really think . . . ?"

"Unless you want to spend your time telling pushy little hacks that you've no idea where Soppy is and no intention of visiting the Argentine yourself and to the best of your knowledge our own marriage is in reasonable nick. Oh, and try and remember to ring Joan later this morning in case anything new's come up. You won't be able to get hold of me — I'm dishing out colours to one of my regiments."

"Wearing uniform?"

"For your sake, darling."

"Excellent. Remember to ask for pictures."

Piers left, rubbing his hands like a miser in a melodrama. Albert hadn't been joking — he did have a kink about women in uniform and kept a scrap-book of his wife and female in-laws on parade. Soppy was really his favourite. Louise grinned, then shook her head as she wondered whether Soppy would ever wear uniform again. Time, she felt, had done another irrevocable trundle. The rules had changed, the angles of illumination shifted. Oh, bring back yesterday . . .

*

80

In the Daimler Louise flipped through the newspapers. The original hack had been working for *Today*, so they had the story across four pages. The rest had botched something together for their later editions. SOPHIE GOES ARGIE yelped the *Sun*. The *Independent* and the *Telegraph* chuntered about the constitution. By now the hyena-pack would be at Heathrow, knocking back scotches as they waited for their flight — this time tomorrow they'd be in the Argentine. The local hacks would be on Soppy's trail already. Father would have asked Bert to get onto her and tell her to come home, or at least to go back to Florida. Bert would agree to try. Soppy would say no. A snapping point? Awful for Bert. He must have known, must have . . .

The telephone bipped. Carrie listened and passed it across. Joan.

"Don't tell me," said Louise.

"It's not that bad, ma'am. I've had Commander Tank on. He's been getting a lot of calls about your schedule for today, so it looks as if you'll have to expect extra camera crews. He's getting on to the adjutant to see if he can lay on some Falkland veterans for you to be photographed talking to . . ."

"There isn't room on the time-table."

"If you cut eight minutes off the crèche visit and get to the mess four minutes late and don't have photos at the crèche which means you go there in uniform and change after . . ."

"While I'm feeding the brat? This isn't music-hall. Oh, all right. How's the Commander taking things."

"All guns blazing."

"OK. Too late to mess around anyway, but give him a ring soon as you can and see that he understands I'm not going to have him casting me as good girl to make up for Soppy being bad girl. It'll only get her deeper in the shit."

"I said that. I'll tell him again, from you."

With an inward shrug Louise passed the handset back. Poor old Tank. He'd spent — how long? — fifteen years at least acting as a kind of heat-shield to the Family, absorbing as much as he could of the otherwise unendurable friction of public curiosity into himself and his office, liked and laughed at by both sides, bluff, decent, another loyal servant. Time he went, too?

81

There were extra camera crews all right, a score of high-paid technicians waiting in sleety drizzle to record the Daimler swinging through the toy-fort gates in case that was all they got. But for Soppy's escapade there might have been just one from the local station, provided nothing more enthralling was afoot in the area. Louise turned to Janine.

"You'd better pick him up," she said. "It's all right — someone will have a brolly. Mr Dyce will bring the cot. Try to hold him so the cameras can see him, but not as if you were doing it on purpose, sort of half in the background. Lady Caroline will ask someone to give you a chance to ring your parents, so you can tell them to watch the one o'clock news — we're pretty certain to be on. If he yells, let him. They'll love that."

He didn't. Louise wondered whether she mightn't have told Janine to pinch him and stimulate an outburst — remind everyone that they couldn't ask for fairy-story-prince behaviour all the time. The whole visit was tense with Soppy's unhintable doings. The regiment had lost men on the hills above Port Stanley. The drizzle, still spiced with sleet, densened through the parade. Normally Louise would have let someone hold a brolly over her, but today she refused. Despite what she'd told Joan to say to Commander Tank it now seemed to her important that she should show that she was prepared to endure in this trivial way what the marching men endured. Objectively it was quite ridiculous that by sitting on a horse in a fancy-dress female version of a nineteenth-century colonel's uniform which reeked of wet labrador as the rain soaked in while lines of similarly soaking and reeking men tramped past to the thump and hoot of a band and the heads clicked round to stare at you and you answered by crooking your arm and holding the flat of your hand towards them under the peak of your kepi, you should be signalling to them and to anyone else watching, "Forget about my sister-in-law who seems to you to have gadded off on a self-indulgent jaunt among the people who killed your friends, because the real nation expresses through me at this moment our understanding of what you feel about their deaths," but that was what happened. It was not a pleasant experience, either physically or emotionally. Louise tried to cheer herself up by wondering whether Piers would get an additional or a diminished kick from seeing her uniform soaked through. She doubted whether dark green serge worked the same way that a wet swimsuit did.

Carrie, typically, had got someone to find a hairdresser among the watching wives. The adjutant had come up with a genuine Falklands widow instead of veterans; though obviously a cheerful woman by nature, and just about to re-marry, she wept painfully during the meeting. Louise was used to having this effect on people, but this particular interview was made more stressful by the knowledge that the moment it was over the hyaenas would pounce and devour every scrap the woman had to offer, so it was impossible to say any more to her than the usual hateful stock of royal banalities. The presence of the pack — their demands not allowed for in the original time-table — jammed the visit tight. What got cut out was any moment of rest or quiet or human contact. Feeding Davy had to be done while the hairdresser patted and combed, and he then had to be dumped straight over to Janine for the burping and cuddling and talking-to, which Louise enjoyed doing for herself.

"You must be whacked," said Carrie as the Daimler slid away.

"I'm all right. Did you get a squint at the news?"

"Janine did."

"You looked lovely, ma'am. It really didn't matter about the rain."

"Did they say anything about the Princess of Wales?"

"Oh, yes, that came first, but it wasn't . . . I mean just old clips of people playing polo, and some snaps of these friends she's with. I'm sure she's having a nice time, ma'am."

Louise smiled. Joan would have taped the news. Janine wouldn't know what to look or listen for.

She was in the bath when the telephone rang.

"Tell them I can't," she called, and continued her game with Davy, cradling his head in the water with her hands and letting buoyancy take care of the rest of him while he threshed his limbs in galvanic uncoordinated jerks, adding his gurgles of delight to the splashes and blinking with amazement when the water chose to hit back at him. For Louise this was the best part of the day, the communication of eye and smile and voice, the touch of his slithering soft flesh on her flesh, things of simple and unarguable importance, natural and true, nothing like the social and moral complexities of life with clothes, let alone uniform, on.

Janine tapped on the door and put her head round, but not far enough to see the scene in the bath. She was a pleasantly prudish little thing.

"It's His Majesty, ma'am."

"Oh, bring the bloody thing in, then. You'll have to take the brat."

There was a moment of fluster as they made the exchange.

"Hello? Lulu? What was that about?"

"Nearly dropped you in the bath. I was teaching your grandchild to swim."

"You must be feeling a bit drowned yourself."

"I had layers and layers on. Smelly though."

"Don't I know it. You came over pretty well. I gather you weren't happy about Tank fixing you up to talk to that Falklands widow? It looked all right."

"It was. In itself, I mean. I just want everyone to understand I'm not going to do anything which makes life harder for Bert and Soppy. I'm not going to be stood alongside her for comparison. We've got to help them sort themselves out. That's what matters."

"One of the things that matter."

"The main thing."

"Perhaps. But I think Tank was right this time — at least till we know what's happening."

"What *is* happening? Did Bert get onto her?"

"The Lipchitzes appear to have told their servants to tell everyone they are away. They'll have half the Argentine press at their gates by now, and our own lot due any moment."

"Did Bert know she was going?"

"Yes. Said it was his idea. I managed not to yell at him if you're interested."

"Well done. What happened to her detectives, by the way? They went to Florida with her, didn't they?"

"Of course. But she was staying there on one of those

spreads with its own security fences, so the arrangement was they didn't hang around while she was inside the ring. Her hosts say she asked to borrow a car and told them not to tell our people — they assumed she was going to visit some man — they seem a pretty easy-going bunch, used to that sort of thing. She'd not got anything much laid on for next day so she could get over her jet-lag before polo started, so they didn't begin to worry till the evening. I may say, if that's how it was, then she's behaved extremely badly towards them. The media over there are beginning to kick up a stink."

"It was a private visit."

"My foot. Polo matches. Princess of Wales playing. People who've never even seen the game would have been driving in from hundreds of miles away. She must have known."

"It just shows how pushed she must be feeling."

"Best hope is she's nipped off to the Argentine for a couple of days to prove she can, and she'll show up in Florida again."

"No. I think she'll do another bolt. The Lipchitzes will help her, won't they? They're so rich they're used to doing whatever they like, so they think everyone should be able to. It's a game to them. They'll pass her on to someone else and tell everyone she just drove off and they don't know where she's gone."

"Oh, God! And the Argentine government are already looking around for ways to exploit it. You know, this is the most bloody awful potmess we've been in since . . . I don't know when."

"How did you get on with Mrs T.?"

"Well as could be expected. No, better than that. We keep it pretty formal, and she's too experienced by now to try and take advantage of something like this until she can be sure where the actual advantage lies. Meanwhile she's got to cope with the usual bloody little ticks on the back benches trying to get themselves a bit of publicity at Question Time. We're putting out a statement for tonight's news . . . "

"I've got to go to the flicks."

"Yes, of course. This Emperor thing. Just like home life, I should think. Listen, I haven't rung you just to blast off — there's something else. When did you last see Bea Surbiton?"

"Can't remember. Bit after Christmas. Why?"

"She's still sitting on my mother's bloody papers. We've been letting it slide, deliberately. The longer Bea muddles around the more time it gives us to deal with your friend Dr Romanov."

"What do you mean, deal with?"

"Don't ask. Nothing sinister, Lulu. He's a tougher nut than we realised. Anyway, you leave him to us. The point is the papers Bea's got. We've got to get them out of her before they get into the wrong hands. It has now become urgent."

"Because of Soppy? I remember Granny . . ."

"You only saw a fraction of it. She tended to behave herself with you, for some reason."

"She was pretty good hell when I was trying to marry Piers."

"That was mild, compared. She regarded that as one in the eye for Bella and me, so she just went in for minor bits of havoc. But there's bound to be stuff in her papers about Soppy and Bert, pure malice, lies, distortions, fantasies . . . can you imagine what it would be like if any of that came out now?"

"You want me to try again with Aunt Bea?"

"Point is, she's got herself in the clutches of some woman, Mrs . . . Mrs . . . I'm getting senile."

"Walsh."

"That's right. Husband was a curious chap my grandfather picked up and gave a job to. Nothing much on his file, but Jane got onto old Lady Godstone — before your time, before mine, even — and she says she remembers him as a fat jumpy little man who played snooker with my grandfather. Wasn't up to his job always, she says — that's code for getting drunk — but he'd got a Russian wife who kept him going. No family."

"I thought there was a daughter."

"Code again. Lady Godstone would've meant he didn't come from anywhere. No connections. Not even a gent, quite likely, but then my grandfather liked a bit of low life — he'd really have been happiest running a back-street pub, only he wouldn't have been mentally up to it. Pot-boy, maybe. You're right about the daughter, though. Lady G. mentioned her specifically, because it was the only point she could think

86

of in his favour. The kid was Down's syndrome, and the wife hadn't any time for her, but Walsh himself was very good with her. Used to push her about the Park in a pram. Lady G. hinted that there was something fishy about the pair of them, but my grandfather wouldn't hear a word against him and my mother approved of her, so they stayed on. Might be useful to know what Lady G. was talking about."

"He'd written a book about his Russian adventures and sent a copy to Great-grandfather, who gave him a job because of being a rabid anti-Bolshie. Then it turned out that the book was stolen from a lot of other books. I think the Walshes may have worked out that if it was published they'd lose his new job because of the hullabaloo, so they got it withdrawn and the publisher went bankrupt. It's a bit late if you're thinking of using that to put pressure on Mrs Walsh to get her claws out of Aunt Bea. By the way, don't Down's syndrome children die young?"

"Yes — that's to say they haven't got proper immunities and tended until recently to succumb to various infections. Why?"

"The daughter's still alive. She must be getting on seventy."

"Can't be, not if she was Down's syndrome."

"According to Mrs Walsh she lives abroad."

"Might be something else, I suppose. Of course Lady G. wouldn't have said Down's syndrome — she'd have said Mongol. Alkaptunuria ? Turner's syndrome? Kleinfelter's? I don't know. If she'd only seen the kid in the pram . . ."

"She might be lying. I think she is about her family name."

"Why on earth?"

"That's my timer. I've got to get out and start dressing."

"Hold it. Let's get this sorted. You are going over to see Bea and Mrs Walsh . . . when?"

"I don't keep my diary in the bath. I'll have to let you know. Have we got any money?"

"What do you mean?"

"Mrs Walsh is helping Aunt Bea because she can read Russian. A lot of Granny's letters are in Russian. Aunt Bea's paying her. She hasn't got a bean on her apparently. That's why she's spinning the job out."

"She'll have a Palace pension. It won't be much."

"I thought we might offer to review it, if she'll let go of the papers. I wouldn't put it that bald."

"Um. Sam won't like it."

"She's been living off scraps from the tourist restaurant according to Aunt Bea."

"It can't be that bad, even for a pre-war pension. They were reviewed in 'fifty-eight and they've been index-linked since 'seventy-two."

"I'm just telling you what Aunt Bea said. I must go. Oh, I'll need to know how things are between the old girls and Alex Romanov. Jane might know. Last I heard he was getting a bit frustrated and beginning to talk about solicitor's letters."

"Can't have that. I suppose . . ."

"I've got to go. Ask Jane and get her to ring me. Oh, and tell Sir Sam to take it easy with Alex. He's pretty jumpy—he told Piers he'd been vetted, and told me he'd put his copies of the letters in a bank. OK? See you soon, I hope. And I hope Soppy comes out of this all right."

"Hope we all do. Enjoy the film, darling."

Slant, whipping sleet-flurries. Large crowd waiting behind barriers in the bitter cold, further away from the entrance than usual. Wet paving, wet cars, wet brollies, wet functionaries, all glittering in the flashlight dazzle. Police tall shadows beyond the brightness. Cheers. Climb from the car, turn, wave, smile. Huddle snugly into white fur collar as you wait for Piers to climb out, laugh as you take his arm, turn again and teeter towards entrance, giving glimpses of wicked crimson stocking through slit of white satin sheath (soft royal porn-limit), on into foyer, shake hands and chat with actors (biogs mugged up in car), joke about court life, smile, look happy, excited — all genuine tonight, because Piers with you, but all part of the job too, along with getting soaked and frozen on colour-parades, signalling to the few million people who happen to be watching between the football results and the weather forecast (no, not in the normal royal spot tonight, but right up front, thanks to Soppy), *Look at me. Think me a dream. Love me.* Yuck.

At least it was a film Louise would have chosen to see anyway. Five years ago she and Albert had staged a Palace revolution and announced that if they were made to attend any more idiot Brit comedies or limping Bond-clones they would yawn publicly the whole way through — there were specialist hacks who came to royal premières with night-vision glasses and never looked at the screen all evening. She was seated out of reach of Piers, so they couldn't hold hands, though Joan must have told them ("HRH greatly prefers . . . "), but the message hadn't got through. Piers wouldn't mind as much as she did, and it would upset him if she made a fuss, so she sat in the lonely dark and half-dozed after the long day. The extraordinary story on the screen became her dream, distortions of familiar sights and events, with the plot a sort of afterthought imposed by the drowsing mind as it automatic-ally tried to assemble the surreal images presented to it into a rational sequence. When the baby emperor marched down between the kowtowing courtiers he became Davy, not just in fancy but in the momentary solidity of dream really, painfully so, with herself watching, powerless to cry out or warn or arrest in any way that happy confident strut towards . . . She must really have been dozing at that point, because in another shift of the dream–pattern, though the strut remained and the child was still her Davy, it was a different Davy, his face Chinese-looking, mongoloid. He was marching through an immense empty courtyard, with ruined walls. He was Down's syndrome . . . Her shudder shook her awake and she forced herself to make sense of the story, but even as she did so she was aware that for quite a time to come, and especially when she met Mrs Walsh, she was going to be haunted by the image of that other baby, of its birth, of its being carried newly born through the mountain passes — why hadn't they left it to die among the rocks? Not realised, either of them, what they'd got? — and then other images of its being wheeled in an immense pram through Kensington Gardens by a fat little ex-adventurer who drank too much and yet loved it. She'd never get Mrs Walsh to talk about it, she realised. The daughter "lived abroad". Or perhaps that was just a euphemism, the sort of thing people like Mrs Walsh might say rather than admit the shame of having to keep their child in a home. And she still said it, from habit, though the child had died years ago. Perhaps.

Punctuality of departure, Father used to say, was as important an aspect of the politeness of princes as that of arrival. If you linger on, everyone else has to, on their best behaviour instead of whooping it up. So you let yourself be whisked away, smartish, three or four hands to shake, no cameras to flirt with, only the small and dedicated group of royal-spotters still waiting at the barriers for a second glimpse. Louise checked quickly to see if her good-luck couple were there. They showed up at almost every announced appearance she made within thirty miles of London, late middle-aged, the woman taller than the man, both in Sunday best, nodding and muttering to each other as she passed, know-ledgeable as judges at a vegetable show. Once she had paused and said hello. They had been polite but reserved. That was not part of the relationship they wanted — to them it had been as if a prize onion had answered back. Anyway the lighting was too patchy tonight for Louise to be sure if they were there. No omen.

3

"Do we have to have that thing on?"

"There's going to be a statement. I'll turn it so I can just hear Big Ben."

"You sound a bit low."

"A bit."

"Not a good point at which to see that particular film."

"I don't know. We're completely different. Well, almost completely. I mean, what was he doing? For anyone? At least we're working, in a sort of way. People still want us. Sometimes I wonder if we aren't a sort of dream everyone's having. If you don't dream at all — I know a lot of people don't think they dream, but they still have . . . what's it called, sounds like some kind of medal?"

"R.E.M. Rapid eye movement."

"That's right. So they are dreaming, only they don't remember, and if they didn't have dreams they'd be off their rockers. But nobody actually knows what dreams are for. Nobody knows what we're for, either, only we're needed. Do computers dream?"

"Not yet. There's probably someone working on it."

"Dogs do, but . . . hang on."

" . . . at midnight on Thursday the twenty-fifth of February. It has been announced from Buckingham Palace that Her Royal Highness the Princess of Wales is currently on a short private visit to friends in the Argentine. His Majesty's Government had of course been consulted about the arrangements, and it had been agreed that in view of the current absence of diplomatic relations with the government of Argentina and also to protect the Princess from intrusion, the visit should be made in a purely private capacity, incognito. It was very much hoped that the media would respect that privacy. Here is our court correspondent . . . "

Nothing much there. A bit more from Mr Reynolds, at least between the lines. Foreign Office ambivalent, Prime Minister clearly not happy, Soppy's determined character, adverse comments in American media . . .

"Are they going to want us to go to the States to make up?"

"Don't know. It'll mean scrapping things here."

"Just don't let it happen in the second week of September. There's a conference in Baku I want to go to."

"We could . . . you mean you'd come to the States with me?"

"And you could come to Baku with me."

"Goodness, I'd simply love to. But the FO would never let me . . . "

"Now that Soppy's broken the trail?"

"That's quite different. She's having a breakdown. Or worse."

"Do you really think so?"

"I had a sort of nightmare during the film. I was still watching it, I think, but I thought I was watching Davy. I really couldn't bear it if they decided he'd better inherit instead of Vick."

"That's absurd. Old Lady Whatsit . . . "

"Bakewell. She wasn't that old. I bet that's why Father is in such a tizz about Granny's letters. They'll be full of stuff about madness running in Soppy's family, dire warnings and so on. I know Mother wasn't altogether happy about it either — she's pretty superstitious about some things — you remember when Davy turned out to be a boy she said it showed you had good blood in your family?"

"I still think it's absurd. Nobody's going to pay any attention to what your grandmother said."

"Haven't you learnt yet? It's a news story. At the very least it'll put extra pressure on Soppy and Bert. Some rag is bound to dig up an expert who'll say going dotty runs in Soppy's family after all, and then that'll put another lot of pressure on Vick while he's growing up, and then you only want one more thing to go wrong — I mean suppose Soppy doesn't get better, for instance? — and then you'll have serious people beginning to say it isn't worth the fuss and why not make a clean break by going straight on to Davy?"

"Who's to say there are not all sorts of hereditary horrors in my family?"

"They won't think about that. Anyway, the first thing I've got to do is nip over to Hampton Court and have a proper shot at getting Aunt Bea to cough up Granny's papers before Alex gets them out of her. I've got a hole Tuesday. I kept it clear because Davy's due a jab, but I don't have to be here."

"What arguments do you propose to adduce?"

"It's Mrs Walsh, really. I think I can get the Palace to up her pension, which might help. The trouble is I don't think she's just being difficult for the money. I can't even threaten her much. She must have read Granny's papers by now, and she'll know she's got things to threaten back with. I think I can manage Aunt Bea, if I can get to talk to her alone. I suppose it'd be easier dealing with Mrs Walsh alone, too."

"Issue a royal command."

"I'm serious."

"So am I. Pull rank. From what you tell me my impression is of someone who makes a parade of being very much *ancien régime*. If she were to refuse a direct request from you she would be partially destroying that self-image."

"I'll think about it. I hate taking that sort of line, if I can help it."

"Glad to hear it."

"Let's talk about something else. I wish I could remember what else I've got on in the second week of September."

"You said the Foreign Office wouldn't let you come."

"I'm going to make them, somehow."

MARCH 1988

I

"That you?"

" . . . "

*"Got anywhere? God, I'll be glad when this is over. I'm sick
with myself I ever got into it."*

" . . . ?"

*"No. I'll see it through. You know me. But it won't be long now,
and I'm telling you if you don't take this chance while you've got it
then I'm going to Security after all. I've shown you a way of getting
what you want, without anyone getting hurt . . . "*

" . . . "

*"I don't care. Better you and me than people who've done nothing
wrong: I'm not having that on my conscience the rest of my life. So
listen. They're in a hurry now to get those papers back out of
Hampton Court. You been reading about the other Princess?"*

" . . . "

*"That's right. And that's why they're shit-scared now about the
papers. Baby's due his first jab tomorrow, and she'd kept it clear to be
with him, but now she's decided she's got to go over . . . "*

2

Since it had been Louise herself who had first asked if the
officer in charge of her personal security could be a woman it
was difficult now to suggest a change, but she had never been
comfortable with Inspector Yale, a sturdy, square-faced
thirty-five-year-old with naturally brassy hair. She sensed
that the Inspector, though giving few tangible hints of it,
regarded her present job as irrelevant both to her career and to

the serious business of police-work, and who was Louise to say that she was wrong? She was efficient, calm and polite, but nuances meant nothing to her. When Louise had tried to suggest to her the best way of handling Piers, she had found herself talking about him as if he were a sulky and unstable teen-age lout.

"We'll do our best not to intrude unnecessarily, ma'am," the Inspector had said.

"I'm sure you will, but . . ."

That *but* still hung in the air between them at their fortnightly meetings. Like Mother but unlike Albert and Father, Louise preferred to see her staff individually, instead of sitting down with everyone together to thrash the future through.

"Anything special in the green diary?" said Louise. "You've been through it with Joan?"

"Of course, ma'am. Mrs Pennycuik asked me to check with you about the visit to Reading General Hospital on the eighth."

"That's only next week. That must be all fixed."

"In consequence of the public reaction to the visit of the Princess of Wales to Argentina we would prefer to move up to an A3 security level — with your consent, of course, ma'am. The agreed timings were only on the basis of a B1 security team."

"You want to cut something out?"

"We shall have to. Besides, there is the likelihood of additional television crews, who will need . . ."

"Oh, God. All right. Fix it with the hospital and tell Joan and the others what you're doing. Try and keep the crèche, and as much of the talking-to-nurses and so on as you can. Those are the things the admin bods will want to chop, so they can keep their own share. If they do, talk about publicity . . . Oh, the hell with it — tell them it's what I want. OK? Now, blue diary. I'm going over to visit Lady Surbiton again this afternoon — that's all fixed. Saturday I'm here. Sunday, chapel at Windsor and then lunch with my parents. We'll take Davy and Piers will drive me in the Rover . . ."

"Under A3 you and Lord Chandler travel separately, ma'am."

"Well, we're not going to. We don't see enough of each other as it is. I mean, if it was a bomb scare, or something, but just because my sister-in-law . . . There's a limit to the strain you can put on family life."

The pale, hard eyes glanced up from the note-book. Strain? they said — servanted, moneyed, shielded, secretaried, adulated? At Louise's age Inspector Yale had been facing knife-bearing yobs in the streets and fending off macho sergeants in the station.

"I'm sorry," said Louise. "When I said OK about going up to A3 I was just thinking about public engagements. A3 is pretty well the whole shoot, isn't it, an absolute cavalcade?"

"Police cars preceding and following the passenger vehicles, and up to six outriders, depending on circumstance."

And half of them with guns, thought Louise. You didn't ask about that sort of thing.

"Well I'm not having that for family jaunts," she said. "I simply don't see the point. It only draws extra attention. People don't like it if they see it, they think it's a waste of policemen who ought to be out catching rapists. Look, let's compromise. I won't whinge about going up to A3 for public engagements, but anything private, things that haven't been announced, when only you and me and Joan know what I'm up to, we'll stay down at B. OK?"

"Your attendance at chapel on Sunday has been announced by Commander Tank's office."

Of course, thought Louise. And there'd be cameras there. The Family sticking up for family values. Sightseers too. The media excitement was at a frenzy — half the press corps must be out on the pampas by now, and not one of them had caught a glimpse or whisper of Soppy. Albert hadn't heard either, Mother said.

"Oh, all right," she said. "You can lay on the troops if you want. But Piers and Davy and I are going in our own car. And things like visiting Lady Surbiton we'll stay right down at B. Just Mr Dyce with me, and the other car tagging along."

Inspector Yale didn't respond for a second or two, but sat staring at her pad, then made a note.

"About Lady Surbiton, ma'am. This will be your third visit since November."

"Oh, God. No. I absolutely refuse. Once a month isn't that often. I've just got one little bit of business to get fixed up — I might even get it finished today . . . "

"But about Lady Surbiton herself . . . "

"Aunt Bea! You can't be serious!"

"I understand she has a grandson . . . "

"Oh, Tim. He's a dead loss, but he's out of harm's way now. He's in gaol in Japan, some kind of hopeless crazy fraud. I wouldn't put anything past him, but he's not due out for at least two more years."

"I believe Lady Surbiton writes to him regularly. It has been suggested that you should ask her not to mention your visits. He may have associates."

"Oh. OK. I must say it seems pretty far-fetched, but if you really think . . . Anyway Aunt Bea won't mind. She's convinced that everything that goes wrong for him is the result of him keeping bad company."

"There is also a Mrs Walsh, Lady Surbiton's neighbour."

"What's wrong with *her*, for heaven's sake?"

Inspector Yale unfolded a flimsy typed sheet and glanced through it. Her expressionless rubbery lips pursed.

"She appears to have been somewhat uncooperative."

"Look, Hampton Court is full of old biddies and codgers. The fact that they've worked at the Palace or been ambassadors or things like that doesn't mean that some of them don't get a bit dotty, like any other lot that age. Actually Mrs Walsh has got her head screwed on more than most, I'd have thought. What do you mean uncooperative?"

"She refused to admit a search team to her apartment."

"Search team? Sniffer-dogs and things? Why on earth . . . "

"We are now at A3, ma'am. The fact that this was to be your third visit . . . "

"You went up before you'd talked to me about it?"

"We thought it for the best, ma'am. In view of the circumstances."

Louise stared at her. She could feel the tension of fury in her neck and shoulder-muscles, but she knew the Inspector would be unaware of it. If you've been born with the knack of self-control and had it reinforced by a childhood of training, even professionals can't see though the mask. Father would have talked to Sir Sam about Granny's papers, and persuaded him to let Louise see what she could do, but Sir Sam's whole instinct would have been to put it into the hands of the professionals. They would have taken the excuse of Louise's impending visit for this preliminary recce. And then what? Supposing Louise got nowhere? A break-in? The trouble was, they were just like real criminals — they always managed to persuade themselves they wouldn't get caught. Think of the mess if they did. Hamptongate. But when they got the bit between their teeth . . .

"Well, it's done now," she said. "I expect you didn't like it either, only you're not allowed to say. Let's get on. The rest of the week's solid green . . ."

It is extraordinary how a stance or gait can snag the unattending eye. Louise was turning onto the bridge at Hampton Court, concentrating, she thought, on leaving room for an express delivery bike to weave past her, when she spotted Mrs Walsh on the pavement. The Rover was already past the spot before she realised who it was, but she didn't need to crane round and check. She was sure. She indicated and pulled in.

"The lady with the stick and the shopping-bag," she said. "I want a word with her anyway."

John Dyce nodded and slipped out, closing and locking the door. In the main-mirror she saw her escort car drawn awkwardly in at the corner, and then in the wing-mirror watched John approach Mrs Walsh and speak. Mrs Walsh stared at him, her whole attitude expressing an almost passionate reserve and self-control, a rejection of any world in which unknown men, however well-mannered and tidily dressed, were permitted to accost her in the street unasked. After a moment's pause she nodded. John offered to carry the plastic bag, but she refused and came stumping towards the car. She was wearing the same clothes as always, including the fabulous brooch. Perhaps it was not the risk it seemed — what mugger or bag-snatcher would guess it was anything more than glass? Louise leaned over and unlocked the door, but let John open and hold it for Mrs Walsh, who for the first time hesitated, as if looking for a running-board to step onto. She allowed John to take her by the elbow and half-turn her, and then help her lower herself into the passenger-seat.

"You looked as if you could do with a lift," said Louise.

"Your Highness is more than kind," said Mrs Walsh.

She seemed to have put on an extra layer of formality to face the outside world, or perhaps she was just cold — she had chosen to make her expedition on this bitterish day without a coat. The effect of her being an emanation from the past was enhanced by a powerful odour of mothballs, presumably coming from her shopping-bag. The whole encounter couldn't be luckier, Louise thought. She had been looking forward with some apprehension to the problem of separating the two old ladies, so that she could tackle Aunt Bea about the papers without the stiffening presence of Mrs Walsh, and then put the Palace's offer about her pension to Mrs Walsh in private.

"You're very spartan," she said, as she eased the car away. "I suppose this doesn't count as cold by Russian standards."

"When I was a child we went to Monte Carlo for the winter."

"That must have been fun."

"We travelled in our own four rail-coaches. When we needed to wait for a connection the servants would haul scenery out onto the platform and dress up and put on plays to entertain us."

"Goodness. It's awful to think how only a few years later you were having to make that frightful journey across Siberia. Did you get the book? I expect you wrote, but my secretary mightn't have showed me."

"I wrote to His Majesty expressing my deep gratitude."

"It was just lucky we still had that last copy. Look, I hope you don't mind, but I've got to talk to Aunt Bea about something in private."

"Of course."

"But there's something I want to talk to you about too — I've got a suggestion to make, if you'd be interested. I'll ring your bell, if that's OK."

"The bell is out of order, but if you knock on the door I will be waiting."

"Terrific. I must say it's marvellous that you and Aunt Bea seem to have hit it off so well. We were desperately worried about her when my grandmother died."

"Beatrice is more able to care for herself than some people realise."

"I've often thought that too. Hold it a moment — Mr Dyce has to check that there aren't any maniacs waiting for us with hatchets . . ."

They shared the lift, but in silence and the odour of mothballs.

"See you later," said Louise, as Mrs Walsh let herself in through her door, and was answered by the usual courtly minibow. That door closed as Aunt Bea's opened.

"My dear, how good of you to come. Maria has gone shopping, but will be back any moment."

"She's here. I saw her on the bridge and gave her a lift."

"Oh, but . . ."

Aunt Bea peered into the shadowy lobby as if expecting to find Mrs Walsh somehow hidden there.

"Let's go and make a cup of tea," said Louise. "I hear you've had a visit from the spy-catchers. I hope they were polite."

"Perfectly, I'm glad to say, only terribly, terribly thorough. But that dog, an absolutely lovely black labrador, so clever! It snuffled around everywhere. Of course I don't have any bombs. I don't think I ever have had. But then, do you know, it became quite excited by the bottom drawer of the bureau, which doesn't have anything in it except old Christmas cards, and we were all greatly puzzled until I remembered that that was where Jack used to keep his machine-gun. He brought it out of the army, you see — of course he wasn't allowed to, but he never worried about things like that. He said he was keeping it to use when the Reds tried to take the country over, but luckily we never needed it. Don't you think that's marvellous, being able to smell the gunpowder after all those years?"

"I'm sorry you had to put up with it. I'm afraid it's part of the system."

"But I enjoyed it. Nice young men, and that wonderful dog. It was like having my own little Royal Tournament, all to myself. Maria was very strong-minded. She insisted on seeing their search-warrant, and when they hadn't got one she wouldn't let them through her door. After all, it's not as if you were visiting *her*."

"Good for her. We must all fight for our freedoms."

"I suppose it is all a consequence of this fuss about the poor dear Princess. Such a worry for their Majesties."

When it came to court life Aunt Bea, vague and hopeless though she seemed, could put two and two together. Even the banal adjectives showed how much she understood, and that raised the question of how much she had told Mrs Walsh. Everything, presumably. At least the remark provided an opening.

"Oh, don't let's bother with a pot," said Louise. "A bag in a mug is fine. You're quite right about Mother and Father being worried stiff about Soppy — as a matter of fact that's why Father asked me to come and see you."

"Oh, if only I could help. But it was such a mistake, don't you think? Look what happened to dear Lady Bakewell — I knew her quite well, you know, and there was a definite likeness. HRH was greatly opposed to the marriage."

"Oh, Aunt Bea, you knew Granny better than anyone. Anything she was against was almost certainly a good thing."

"She was very experienced in court matters."

"All she wanted was trouble, especially with Mother and Father."

"I'm afraid that's true, my dear, much of the time. But she was terribly clever how she set about it. If somebody had a weak point, she was sure to find it."

"And that's all she still wants, isn't it? I bet there's some wicked stuff about Soppy in her letters."

"I'm afraid so, my dear. Maria was reading me parts of what she had to say only last evening."

"You see, that's what Father wanted me to come and talk to you about. Of course most of what Granny says is nonsense, but the one thing we can't afford is any of it coming out into the open just now."

"I assure you, my dear, it is all quite safe with me."

"Yes, of course. We all trust you absolutely. But it's still a worry. And, Aunt Bea, it's not just you."

"Who . . . surely you cannot think Maria . . . "

Louise smiled reassuringly. It was difficult to tell someone that on past form they had a hundred-per-cent record in picking losers in the people-to-trust stakes.

"Of course you know her best," she said, "and you're sure she's all right. I know her a bit and I think so too. But Mother and Father don't know her at all, so you can't expect them . . . no, wait a bit . . . that's not really the point. They'd still be worried, whoever had the papers. And according to the will it isn't really supposed to be you at all."

"Oh, my dear, but it is. HRH specifically asked me to take charge of them if anything should happen to her."

"Did she really? You didn't say so last time."

"Didn't I? I know I do get rather muddled, but that's always been quite clear in my mind."

"According to the will, Alex Romanov's supposed to take charge of them."

"Oh, I'm having such a time with that young man! I scarcely dare answer the telephone unless Maria is in the room. I don't know where I should be without her. She is so wonderfully composed and firm — of course she speaks to him in Russian, but I can tell from the tone. And only this week he has employed a solicitor to write to me in a really most abrupt manner. I do find that sort of thing so un-settling."

"Poor Aunt Bea. Have you talked to Jane Gordon-Byng?"

"Oh, yes, more than once. I'm sure she is doing her best, but all she will say is that I must send her all the papers and then she will deal with Count Alex."

"Yes, that's right. That would be much the best."

"But she doesn't speak Russian."

"She'll get someone from the Foreign Office, or some-thing. Please, Aunt Bea, can't you see . . . "

"Oh dear . . . Maria . . . "

Aunt Bea had half-turned, as if expecting to find Mrs Walsh standing beside her to support her toppling resolution. Louise sensed an inward squaring of shoulders.

"I can't, you see," said Aunt Bea.

"Can't?"

"I promised."

"Promised Granny?"

"Well. Yes."

"That you wouldn't let the Palace have her papers?"

"Yes."

"What were you supposed to do?"

"Do? Look at them, and then . . . oh dear . . ."

"Give them to Alex Romanov? That's what it says in the will."

"Yes, that's right. Only after I'd looked at them and taken out the ones which might hurt people's feelings. *That's* why it's so important Maria should help me read right through them first."

"What about the others, the ones you didn't pass on?"

"Well, burn them, I suppose."

(No, that was inconceivable. Or that Granny would have trusted the despised Aunt Bea with such a task, or indeed imagined that she herself wouldn't outlive the poor old thing. Bloody woman. Women.)

Louise kept her face of concern, and apparent belief in the fibs she had just been told.

"That does make it tricky for you," she said. "Personally I don't think Granny had any right to ask you to do that. All she wanted was to go on making trouble for everyone after she was dead. I think you've got to grit your teeth and let me take the whole lot off to Jane, and then you can tell Alex Romanov that's what you've done and you won't be bothered any more."

"I can't, my dear. I simply can't."

Aunt Bea was becoming too distressed for Louise to persist on that tack.

"Are you still paying Mrs Walsh for her help?" she said.

"I hope nobody is going to tell me I should not."

"No, of course. It's up to you. Only . . . well, I told Father what you'd said about her finding things a bit tough and he said he'd look into her pension. She's got one, all right. It's pre-war, but it's index-linked now so she ought to just about get by. I mean, she shouldn't be living on scraps from the tea-room."

Silence, and again the sensed stiffening of the will.

"I'm sorry, Aunt Bea."

"You're doing your best, my dear, and really I'm very grateful, but . . . if I tell you something, will you promise not to breathe a word more about it to anyone?"

"I might have to tell Father."

"Oh, I suppose . . . You see, my dear, Maria has a daughter."

"Yes, I know. She lives abroad, she said."

"Exactly, and the reason is that she's a Mongol, poor thing. There's a family who take care of her — it's somewhere quite primitive, because that's the only thing Maria can afford. But that's why she hasn't any money. She's extremely proud about not asking for help, and she would very much prefer not to have to tell *anyone*."

"Yes, I see. But surely . . . "

"It is no use making suggestions. Maria has her own way of doing things. She is so very, very Russian. HRH was very Russian too, of course, but in a different way — Petersburg Russian, if you know what I mean. Maria comes from a good family, but I sometimes wonder if she doesn't actually think more like one of those peasants you read about."

Louise understood at once. It was an example of Aunt Bea's occasional perceptiveness that she should have latched on to something not at all obvious, a sort of primal simplicity, brutality almost, behind Mrs Walsh's courtly façade. Not that the actual courts were really that far from barbarism. Louise remembered Father muttering once during some ceremonial function that a dish-washer service engineer slouched in front of his TV with his Heineken in his hand presented a more civilised spectacle.

"Still," she said, "you see . . . well, actually, Aunt Bea, I don't really believe everything you were telling me just now. No, wait. I think, and Father does too, that the real reason for you trying to hang on to Granny's papers for so long is that you need an excuse for paying Mrs Walsh to help you. You know she wouldn't take it if you just gave it to her. No, I still haven't finished. Father's talked to the Palace about her pension, and they'd be quite happy to top it up a bit if there was a good reason for doing so, like helping pay for her daughter's keep."

"But that's the whole point, my dear. You simply can't tell them that."

"They know already. I mean, they don't know about Mrs Walsh needing help — they didn't even know the daughter was still alive — it's a bit of a medical record, actually — but they do know that she was Down's syndrome. You see the security people had to check on Mrs Walsh — it's a bit like sending the sniffer-dog in here — and they looked in the Palace files and they found somebody who remembered the Walshes back in Great-grandfather's time. Do you understand?"

Aunt Bea's large white face had changed as Louise spoke. For a moment it looked as if she was about to burst into tears with the release of tension.

"Well, my dear . . . " she breathed.

"I mean you can't go on helping her for ever, can you? But if we could get her a pension hike that would be something permanent."

"It would certainly be a solution. The difficulty is going to be to get Maria to ask for anything. She won't like your knowing about her daughter — she won't like it at all."

"I'll just have to do my best to persuade her. Don't worry. She can't eat me."

Louise felt full of confidence as she walked down the hallway and out onto the landing. Things were going really well. Aunt Bea had as good as admitted her real reason for hanging on to Granny's papers, and also seemed to think that a pension hike for Mrs Walsh would do the trick. Mrs Walsh herself now seemed less formidable, partly because of this progress but also because of the quasi-magical power of knowing her real name. Her description of the servants putting on plays for her family while they waited for the next train to hitch the coaches to made it almost certain that her real name had been Belayev, and not Belitzin. Alex had told Louise about the Belayev custom of employing servants who could also act; he'd been fairly insistent that there were no girls of Mrs Walsh's age in the family, but perhaps she had been some kind of poor cousin, a hanger-on — not that poor, though, if there'd been jewels to sell and her mother had given her the great brooch she wore. Trivial mysteries, none of which Louise intended to explore or exploit just now.

She raised the brass knocker, but the door opened before she could bang it. There was then almost a collision in the doorway as Mrs Walsh started forward instead of holding the door for Louise.

"May I come in please?" said Louise.

"It is much warmer in Beatrice's apartment."

"I would rather talk to you in private."

For a moment Mrs Walsh didn't move and seemed as if she wasn't going to. Louise looked her in the eyes and deliberately, without words or gesture, pulled rank.

"Very well," said Mrs Walsh, but instead of standing aside backed off. Louise followed her into the hallway and closed the door. To her surprise she found not the mirror-image of Aunt Bea's entrance which she'd been expecting but a much smaller lobby, with no doors opening from it and only a stairway winding up out of sight opposite the door. Mrs Walsh stood at the bottom of the stairs, blocking further progress. There was one weak bulb overhead, against the left wall a cheap chair with an army greatcoat flung across it, and a worn brown carpet on the floor and stairs. It was indeed icy cold. Mrs Walsh must have been waiting down here, wearing the greatcoat perhaps, while Louise talked to Aunt Bea.

"I'm sorry to barge in on you like this," said Louise. "The thing is, I need your help. First I want to say how grateful we all are — my family, I mean — to you for taking Aunt Bea under your wing the way you have. We really do appreciate it. But we're really worried about the way she's insisting on hanging on to my grandmother's papers. We don't want to hurt her feelings, but she hasn't got any right to be doing it."

"I cannot help. It is Beatrice's own decision."

"Yes, I know. But I think what you can help with is the reasons why she's doing it. Of course she says that it's because my grandmother told her to, but actually I don't believe that. I knew Granny pretty well, and I'm quite sure she wouldn't have trusted Aunt Bea with a job like that. I think Aunt Bea probably had a vague feeling that Granny didn't want the Palace to get their clutches on them which is probably true — that's why she made Alex Romanov her literary executor — but we could easily have persuaded her to give them up if it wasn't that they gave her an excuse for helping you financially, and she just wants to go on doing so as long as she can."

Mrs Walsh said nothing.

"We aren't against that," said Louise. "That part of it's no business of ours — it's her own money — but it isn't very satisfactory, is it? I mean, it can't go on on that basis for ever. I've talked to my father, and he thinks we can come to a better arrangement."

Silence still, but was there a gleam in the greenish eyes?

"They've looked up your husband's file in the Palace," said Louise, "and they've talked to someone who remembers you both . . ."

"Who, may I ask?"

"Lady Godstone."

Mrs Walsh nodded.

"She remembered your daughter," said Louise. "You said first time we met that you'd got one, and that she lived abroad, but it was only after talking to old Lady Godstone that anyone realised that you might need help looking after her. If they'd known, I'm sure they would have done something about increasing your pension ages ago, but . . ."

"Your Highness is entirely mistaken."

The words came out with no anger or appeal, as toneless as a voice from a machine.

"Oh?"

"It is true that I have a daughter. She lives abroad and I contribute to her upkeep. I have always done so, and will continue until one of us dies. I have never asked anyone for help and need none. If Beatrice chooses to pay me for my services, that is her own affair. I see no reason to doubt her word that the late Dowager Princess asked her to behave as she is doing. I cannot, whoever asks me, encourage her to break that trust. The wishes of the dead are to be respected. That is all I have to say."

"I think you're making a mistake, Mrs Walsh. We're not trying to buy you off. We genuinely feel we should help in a case like . . ."

"I need no help. I have needed none all my life. What I have done I have done without help. If you wish, you may come and see how I live."

Without waiting to see whether Louise in fact did wish, Mrs Walsh turned and started to hobble up the stairs, crab-wise, putting her left foot up a step and leaning her weight on her stick while she hoisted her right foot up beside it. The process had the deftness of long practice, and looked almost graceful, as though Mrs Walsh's powerful will was able to impose her own notions of order on the entropy of dissolution into old age. Louise followed her. The cold, if anything, increased as they went up.

The stair-carpet reached only a couple of steps beyond the first turn. After that came bare boards. At the top was a low ceilinged landing, carpetless and bare apart from a small ebony table with one drawer, inlaid with mother-of-pearl. All the doors onto the landing were closed, but Mrs Walsh opened one and held it like a landlady showing prospective lodgers round her boarding house. Beyond the door was a large bare room, directly beneath the roof, to judge by the shape of the ceiling. Two grimy dormers showed the back of the brick crenellations of a parapet. The only furniture was an upright wooden chair beside a black pot-bellied stove in the middle of the far wall. The room was no warmer than the stairs, but smelt faintly of that special kind of rather peppery smoke you get when somebody has been trying to light a fire and failed. There was, in any case, nothing to burn, no log-basket or coke-scuttle.

Louise walked into the room and turned. Mrs Walsh waited at the door. The tour continued. There was a bedroom, containing a bed, table with mirror, and chair, all old and plain; another room, smelling strongly of mothballs, with nothing in it but four old tin trunks against the walls, their lids stencilled "Major J. J. Walsh"; a kitchen with one chair and table and a condemnable gas stove; an icy bathroom with an equally dangerous-looking water-heater. The whole flat spoke of a life as bleak as those lived in the most basic and possessionless mud huts which Louise had been shown in the Sahel, but the inhabitants there had listlessly endured her coming, answered her translated questions in tones of no hope, stared at her with the large but lightless eyes of starvation. Mrs Walsh, though, seemed to vibrate with renewed energies as she hobbled round. The tap of her stick on the gnarled planking was a rattle of triumph. At last she turned and waited with an air of challenge beside the little black table on the landing. Louise felt an impulse to try and put Mrs Walsh off her balance by asking about this. It had an oddity about it. It was ugly but well-made, the only good piece of furniture in the whole flat, and as such seemed to have a symbolic quality, as if asserting something about Mrs Wash and her past life, rather in the way that the diamond brooch did. But this wasn't a game, so she asked the expected question.

"What happened? Was it all in the warehouse with the books?"

"I burnt it in my stove. What I could not burn I took out piece by piece and threw in the river."

Louise stared.

"When you reach my age," said Mrs Walsh, "you cannot know how soon you may die. You must do necessary things while you still possess the strength and will. That is all I am prepared to tell you. I have shown you this so that you may tell your father with what little comfort I am prepared to live. As his loyal subject I am grateful to him for his continued permission to reside here, in recognition of my husband's long service to His late Majesty. As I have said, I need no more help than that. None at all."

She moved aside and waited for Louise to go first down the stairs, but Louise stayed where she was.

"Yes, I see," she said. "I don't understand, I mean, but I suppose I accept what you're telling me. It's very difficult. You see, Aunt Bea really ought not to have Granny's papers. I know she wouldn't do anything to let my family down, and I'm sure you wouldn't either, but it doesn't stop people being extremely jumpy about them being here. You've read a lot of them by now. You know the sort of things Granny said about people. The trouble is, that the rest of us don't know exactly what she said, and there's people in the Palace and the Foreign Office and so on who are already putting pressures on my father to hand the problem over to the security services. I can't tell you what a nuisance that might be, not just to us, but to you and Aunt Bea too. They'll want to come and see you, and ask all sorts of questions, and bother people who used to know you, and so on. The reason I'm here at all is because we've been fighting them off, trying to save Aunt Bea — and you too, of course — that kind of fuss, but I'm afraid if Aunt Bea's going to go on taking that line that's the next thing that'll happen."

Louise had been reasonably sure that Mrs Walsh was going to refuse her first appeal, and so had thought out her line with care; she had spoken in tones of sympathetic worry, and got it about right; but she hadn't expected to enjoy the process. It was the sort of devious, bullying, backstairs work which her ancestors had employed courtiers for, and which had in the end got most other monarchies booted into exile. As it turned out, though, she felt no shame. The tour of the flat had changed her attitude to Mrs Walsh. Previously she had found her forbidding but impressive and, despite the nuisance of her intervention into the imbroglio over Granny's papers, had assumed that it was nice for Aunt Bea to have fallen so quickly into the dependent relationship she needed — anyway, a distinct improvement on Granny. Now she began to wonder whether Mrs Walsh mightn't turn out to be an even worse monster.

Mrs Walsh listened to the speech, nodded a couple of times and tapped her stick on the ground. The cold on the landing seemed to close round them. It struck Louise that there might be a far more basic and straightforward explanation for Mrs Walsh's wish to prolong the sorting of Granny's papers, at least till the summer.

"It must have been desperately cold here in that spell we had in January," she said.

"Your winters are nothing. I have known real cold. I have seen my mother left to die in the snow like a foundered horse, with the dribblings freezing to her cheek."

"How ghastly."

"It is how we were treated."

"Let's go and warm ourselves up with a pot of tea."

Louise was in bed, giving Davy his goodnight feed, when the telephone rang. She picked it up with her free hand and cradled it into her shoulder.

"Lulu? I got a message to call you."

"You owe me a bottle of champagne or something."

"I can spare a Mars Bar. What are we celebrating?"

"Aunt Bea says we can have Granny's papers back."

"Excellent. How did you manage it?"

"I went over and saw her this afternoon. I had a bit of luck, because I spotted Mrs Walsh on the way and gave her a lift, and that meant I got a chance to ask her not to come in while I was talking to Aunt Bea. Anyway Aunt Bea tried to tell me a lot of fibs which Mrs Walsh had put her up to about Granny giving express orders that she had to hang on to the papers, so I trotted off to see Mrs Walsh. I talked to her about the pension, but she wasn't interested — do you know she lives in the most appallingly spartan way, no carpets, no heat, a hard bed, a few kitchen chairs; she showed me to prove she didn't want anything. She's a bit dotty, I think. I'm not sure she's going to be good for Aunt Bea after all. Anyway, when she said no to the pension hike I told her that in that case we'd hand the whole thing over to Security, and they'd start investigating her . . ."

"I trust you didn't put it in those terms."

"Of course not. I said what a nuisance it was going to be for poor Aunt Bea, and just mentioned they'd do Mrs Walsh too while they were at it, but we both knew what I was talking about. Anyway Aunt Bea rang up before I'd even got home and left a desperate sort of message with Joan. Poor old thing. I felt awful when I rang her, listening to her squirming. But the upshot is I'm going over to pick the papers up next week."

"We could send people round."

"I'd rather do it myself. It'll be Janine's day off, so I'll take Davy over and let Aunt Bea hold him. John can carry the heavy stuff. I'll take one of the big cars. It'll be all right. I thought if we just send men round Aunt Bea doesn't even know . . ."

"Well, if you can spare the time."

"Davy will love the ride. And then that'll leave your people free to see what they can do about Alex Romanov. How's that going?"

"Last I heard they were having trouble locating the blighter."

"What does that mean?"

"He's pushed off somewhere. Gone skiing or something."

"I wouldn't have thought he was the type. Piers might know. I'll ask him, soon as he comes to bed. Hold it, I'm just switching the brat to the other barrel. No, don't ring off — I want to know about Soppy . . . OK, ready now. Joan told me you'd found her."

"Yes."

"Well, that's something. You don't sound too happy."

"No. That is to say, from our own immediate point of view, things have perhaps taken a turn for the better. It seems that we all rather misjudged the Lipchitzes. They'd only had the girl in the house a couple of days before they'd cottoned on something was seriously wrong . . ."

"She probably ate a passing steer, or something. Sorry."

"It is far from funny. They had their doctor flown up from B.A., and a nursing team to keep an eye on her. I've talked to the doctor. He knows his stuff. He's doped her pretty thoroughly and we're making arrangements to have her flown home."

"How bad is it?"

"Can't say. These things take a hell of a lot of investigation and trial and error. Most of them are more treatable than they used to be though, but even when you've come up with a treatment you don't always know what went wrong in the first place. She'll certainly need treatment, and there's a very good chance that it will be effective."

"Poor thing. I suppose the next question is, is it the same thing Lady Bakewell had?"

"Whatever that was. Schizophrenia appears to have an hereditary element. We did a pretty thorough investigation at the time, and we couldn't turn up anyone else in the family who had shown signs of instability."

"I sometimes think that you have to be a bit potty to be as unpleasant as Aunt Eloise."

"Power mania is not a recognised disease. It is a normal human condition. You have of course hit on the most serious aspect of the problem, as it concerns us. All I can say is we won't be able to make up our minds until we've been able to form some sort of diagnosis of Soppy's case . . ."

"At least you can let everyone know it was mainly pressure from the bloody hacks that brought it on."

"Do you think so?"

"Well, it must have been."

"Not necessarily, but in any case not what I meant. If we take that line, whether openly or with a leak or two, they'll go on the defensive, and their best line will be that Soppy was mentally unstable from the start and we should never have let Albert marry her. That, of course, is why it's such good news that you've persuaded Beatrice to release my mother's papers. My own view is that there are going to be quite enough busybodies of various kinds taking the line you suggest for us not to need to. We are proud to have a free press and while regretting certain recent excesses blah blah blah."

"And let them tear each other's throats out."

"If we're lucky we might get two or three months of slightly less repulsive manners."

"From some of them, anyway."

"It's about the best we can hope for. Look after yourself, darling."

"Same to you."

Davy had fallen asleep between suck and suck, a bad habit he was supposed to be getting out of. Louise squinted down at the almost abstract shapes, the round cheeks, the round skull, the round of her breast. How long was Father going to live? No guessing — you couldn't help feeling that someone with such a bad temper might pop off any moment. He'd often said he was going to retire when he was sixty-five, like everyone else — in seven years' time that would be — supposing Mrs T. would let him. She intended to be still going by then, and she might regard it as a bad precedent. Let's say he did, Davy would be pushing eight . . . of course it wasn't really going to matter until Albert snuffed it or retired, and by then his two would be in their forties and if they were going off their rockers it would have shown up, surely . . . Only the in-between years, growing up as a might-be-heir, that would be bad . . . worse if he'd been a girl, of course . . .

poor Soppy.

"Oh, come on, you little brute. Wake up!"

In answer to her shake Davy tilted his head away from the breast and snored, the personification of smug male apathy. Briskly Louise swung herself out of the bed, took him back to the nursery, slapped a dry nappy round him and shoved him down into his cot. Of course he would wake in less than an hour in an outrage of wind. Let him.

3

"Not a word. He was supposed to ring me — when was it? Friday."

(They had already talked about Soppy, back and forth, round and round, useless. They had kissed and started to drowse when the grit of a small undissolved duty had grated in the wards of sleep and woken Louise to ask about Alex.)

"What about?"

"Some sort of traffic control project his firm wants to tender for. It involves a bit of math I did a paper on a few years back — too abstruse for anyone on his team, but I've got a student who could do with the money. There's a deadline on the tender, apparently."

"So he hasn't gone skiing."

"Wouldn't have thought so. Most likely they've decided not to use Simon and Alex as a result is locked up with a towel round his head trying to sort out the math himself."

"If you do hear from him will you let Father know?"

"Um."

"It's important, darling. It isn't for us, mainly it's for Soppy."

"Um still. It seems to me not a question of the motive, but what your father — or rather his minions — would then do with the knowledge. I would very much prefer Alex to hand the papers over, but even for Soppy's sake I will not be involved in underhand methods of forcing him to do so. I will if you like explain the position to him and tell him as forcefully as I can that in my opinion he ought to do as you wish."

"My turn to um. I mean, I know it's outside the contract,

114

you going that far. I really appreciate it. The trouble is, if you tell him what's up . . . Do you believe him when he says he's doing all this just out of respect for Granny's wishes?"

"Nobody does anything for a single motive. All actions are the outcome of a series of inner compromises, mainly unconscious. I don't, as a matter of fact, think Alex is very interested in the money, though no doubt it plays a part. If I had to choose a dominant motive, I would guess that, having been brought up as a fringe member of what had once been a dominant family but which itself had been suddenly marginalised by the Russian Revolution, a family whose chief activity must have seemed to a child to be the interchange of minor personal details, Alex would like to be taken seriously as a practitioner in that field."

"I love it when you get to the end of sentences like that."

"He is clearly a skilled gossip. He would like his skill recognised in the publication of a book. If gossip were a degree course — and a lot of them aren't much more — he'd already have a chair and a string of publications to his name."

"So we aren't going to be able to buy him off."

"I wouldn't have thought so. I can tell you from experience that if that is his motive, it is a very strong one."

"Can I tell Father? He'd understand."

"Suggest that he aims for a compromise."

"When they've seen Aunt Bea's collection they'll have a clearer idea what they're talking about."

"You fixed that?"

"I'm going to collect them on Wednesday. I won't tell you how I did it. My methods were underhand, but I wasn't ashamed. I'm still not. I think Mrs Walsh is off her rocker. You remember that book, the one you got Mr Brown to read for me? I told you she'd asked if she could have it because it was the last copy, and I got Mrs Suttery to get permission for me to give it to her — I think she's burnt it. She lives in an almost totally bare flat, no carpets, curtains, just sticks of furniture, no heating except an old stove — she showed me round. She'd been burning paper in the stove. I know it could have been anything. I just have an intuition."

"I have a counter-intuition that I am about to fall asleep."

"Me too. Sleep well."

MARCH 1988

I

"That you? Now listen, because this is the last time I'm calling you. You've got just this one chance, and for both of our sakes you better bloody take it . . ."

2

The Rover came to rest while Louise was still on the carphone. It was a bad spot, blanking the signal completely.

"Hell," she said. "We're too close to the building. I thought brick was OK."

John was leaning across to unbelt the nest-egg. He looked round. "It'll be the scaffolding over on the other wing, ma'am. That's not that far. Shall I back up then?"

"Don't bother. You can do it when I'm out. Joan was trying to check something with me about a change in the Portsmouth visit. Tell her to call me on Lady Surbiton's number — give me a couple of minutes. OK?"

"Very good, ma'am."

He got out, opened the door for her and handed her the nest-egg. Davy woke as the now familiar lift doddered up. When it stopped he would think about yelling, but for the moment the movement kept him happy. He had his Edward VII look strongly today, the heavy eyelids and the rolls of blubber.

"You're a smug, self-satisfied little piglet," said Louise.

He blinked at the sound of her voice and blinked again as the lift bumped to a stop. Louise pushed the inner gate aside, the outer door was opened for her and held by a smiling man in paint-splodged overalls.

"Thank you," she said.

"You're welcome."

As she stepped past him he moved, leaping against her and clamping her body violently to his, pinioning her arms. Her shout was still in her throat when a hand closed over her mouth from behind, another hand forced her head right back till she could no longer clench her jaw shut, and a roll of dry fabric was forced between her teeth and lashed there with a cloth. The nest-egg was prized from her grip. A moment later Davy's scream of fright was muffled, though not stopped. The man who had opened the door for her let go, gripped her left wrist, bent and jerked her over his shoulder in a fireman's lift.

Louise had already gone limp. After Chester Father had insisted on everyone doing a course in how to react if something like this happened. You control the useless urge to struggle and scream, you signal to your attackers any way you can that you're going to do what they want, you wait for help from outside. She even knew what a gag felt like, and how not to choke on it.

The man turned not to Aunt Bea's door but to Mrs Walsh's. It must have been already on the latch. Upside down, under his arm as he carried her up the stairs, Louise caught glimpses of the other man. He had the nest-egg under his arm, and one large hand with a tea towel clamped over Davy's face. The ridiculous little arms and legs threshed against the belts of the nest-egg.

The man carrying Louise strode along the bare boards of the top landing. He twisted to ease her through the door of the main room so that she didn't see what happened to Davy, but she could hear from the muffled yells that he was being taken somewhere else. The man bent and slid her from his shoulder, still holding her wrist and spinning her as she straightened so that he could force her arm up behind her back.

"OK," he said. "One peep or wriggle from you and the baby gets a bullet. Understand?"

Louise nodded.

Three chairs had been placed facing the near wall, behind

the door. Aunt Bea and Mrs Walsh sat in the further two. Louise knew them by the shapes of their bodies and their clothes but their heads were hidden in coloured pillow-cases. Mrs Walsh's grey toque lay on the floor by her chair. Their wrists and ankles were lashed to the chairs. The man pushed Louise to the empty place. She sat without his having to force her down and placed her legs and arms ready.

"Look at the wall and don't move," said the man.

Louise stared at the beige surface. Her ears strained for Davy's voice, still yelling, still muffled, but different now, she thought, not the yells of fresh fright and outrage, but outrage remembered, as if someone was trying to calm him. Not daring to move her head she squinted down over the blur of her cheek at the back of the man's head as he knelt to lash her legs. Close-cropped blond hair, faintly coppery, the glint of the metal earpiece of his spectacles. Purposefully she reconstructed the memory of his face, seen for those two seconds in the dimness of the landing below. She was good at faces. Flattish, snub-nosed, eyebrows strong and level, chin dented but not dimpled. She would know him again.

He rose and stood behind her. She heard the rustle of cloth, but before he pulled the pillow-case down over her head he bent and whispered into her ear.

"All right. Ten minutes and we'll be going. We're taking the kid with us. He'll do — we've got people who know about kids. Then when we're safe away we'll call your police and tell them where you are. They'll come and get you. Now I'm giving you a message for them, so listen. They won't be seeing the kid again, nor will you, nor will anyone, without they do what we'll be telling them. You got that?"

Louise nodded.

"So it's down to you. You see that they play along with us and you'll have your boy back inside of a week, not a hair of his head touched. Right?"

As Louise nodded again the pillow-case slid deftly down over her head. She gazed dry-eyed at the yellow unfocussable blur. Footsteps dwindled across boards. A hinge moaned. She seemed to have nothing inside her but a chilly, timeless hollow, far bigger than her own real body. She tried to think about the time. A couple of minutes, she'd told John. Joan

118

would ring Aunt Bea's, get no answer, wait, try again — the Portsmouth decision was urgent — then ring the car again. Ten minutes, the man had said, and they'd be going, so if Joan didn't call John soon . . . Could she have fought for time, held things up, pretended not to understand what the man was telling her? He would just have thought she was being stupid. Stupid. Oh, they were stupid, these people. Not stupid, blind. Couldn't they see that whatever happened, whatever it was they wanted, they couldn't have it in exchange for Davy? Suppose she'd sold everything she owned — several million pounds it would come to — and offered them that? For herself she'd do it, of course, or given her own life or anything else that was hers to give, but she'd never be allowed to, never. Father, Mrs T., everyone else . . . Couldn't they see that? It was so obvious, but you'd never persuade them. For them the world simply had to be the shape and way they imagined it was so as to justify the things they did, the maimings, the bombings . . . These were weary old thoughts, rehearsed again and again, every time something happened in the news or she did a visit to Ulster. Now they reeled through her head, useless, repetitive, the old imaginary scenes of argument and pleading . . . not that they'd ever give you the chance . . .

Her body leaped in her chair, jerking against the bonds, actually teetering the legs off the ground so that she thought it would topple. By the time it was still the signal that had set it off, Davy's scream of pain, was muffled again. She willed the tension away. What were they doing? Not a hair of his head, the man had said. But they'd have to keep him quiet. Yes, of course, that must have been the needle going in. He loathed jabs. Oh, please, please, let there be someone who knew to get the dose right! Oh, let them be competent, please! Ghastly, cruel, wrong, but not idiots. She drew a deep breath of the dank air in the pillow-case and tried again to relax. The jerking about, the automatic attempt to yell out, had shifted the pad in her mouth, almost choking her. Trying to work it back in its proper place brought a bubble of vomit up. Carefully she swallowed it back down. Davy was still crying. It wasn't one of those instant knock-outs, then. Oh, let them wait, not try a double dose, let them think how much more use he was to them alive . . .

Closer, right in the room, a new noise, the three quick tones of the pager. It had been in her handbag. They must have dropped that in the room somewhere. John would wait, say, a minute, and try again. She counted the seconds. Had they heard? Davy was yelling still, but she could tell from the tone that any moment now he would give up, and between one indrawn breath and the next yell fall with hardly a whimper into darkness. What would John do if she didn't answer this time? There, again the pager, and almost at once hurrying steps on the boards. The pillow-case off, hands at her neck, the gag plucked free, the voice at her ear.

"Someone calling you, then? Careful, now, look straight at the wall. What's up?"

"My secretary was going to ring me at Lady Surbiton's. It was something urgent, so when I didn't answer she must've rung the car and asked my detective where I was. That's him paging me."

"What'll he do now?"

"Try once more, and then probably come and look for me."

"Just the one of him?"

"He'll tell the men in the other car what he's doing."

"How many?"

"Two."

"Got the number for your car?"

"In my Filofax. I think I can remember it."

"Right. I'll call him for you, and you can tell him you're all right. No, wait. We'll have him up here. Give him a reason, tell him to just say to the others he'll be here in the next twenty minutes."

"Yes, I can do that."

"Give us that number, then."

The pager sounded again through the beeps of the portable telephone as the man pressed the keys. Then the usual long wait. Then John's voice.

"Hello."

"Hello," she said. "Princess Louise here."

The name sounded unreal on her tongue. She never used it

herself if she could help it. Surely the man would notice, or notice John's pause . . .

"Uh . . . They've been trying to call you at Lady Surbiton's, ma'am. They want, uh, to know if you've heard anything from Miss Lucy Ford. They're sorry, ma'am, but it might be urgent."

Louise could feel the faint pressure of the man's hand on her hair where he was holding his own head as close as he could to the earpiece. She kept her muscles tense, trying not to signal her relief that John had picked up her breach of the security code, and answered in a way that showed he had.

"Quite urgent," she said. "Tell Mrs Pennycuik I'll call her as soon as I'm free. She couldn't get me at Lady Surbiton's because we're in Mrs Walsh's flat. When you've spoken to Mrs Pennycuik could you come up? We aren't ready yet, but we've got a load of papers to shift. We could do with a strong arm. You could tell the others you'll be about twenty minutes."

"Mrs Walsh's flat, ma'am?"

"The door straight opposite the lift."

"Very good, ma'am. I understand."

"Thanks."

The telephone bipped once as the man switched off. The gag went back in Louise's mouth and the pillow-case slid over her head. She heard quick movements close by but didn't understand them till the man spoke.

"Now, you, lady. We'll have you at the top of the stairs. The door will be on the latch. He'll knock, and you'll call to him to come up. You'll stand by and send him on in here. No tricks. You try anything, and your friend's dead, dead as him next door. Right?"

"I do not know that I can stand," said Mrs Walsh's voice, loud and tremorless.

"I'll help you up. You've got a minute or two yet — he's a call to make. Steady now."

"I shall need my stick."

"Take my arm. There's a table out there, you can hold on to that — keep you in the one place, right."

The footsteps receded. Louise felt her self-control beginning to give. In his hurry the man hadn't pulled the pillow-case right down over her shoulders, and she had to force herself not to try and thresh it free. Her heart thudded. The unusable adrenalin pumped round her bloodstream. Footsteps returned — two men, she thought, waiting just inside the door ready to jump John. What would he have done? Called Security, alerted the other car — there'd be an A1 alert by now, red-red, cars and men flooding in. Then he'd have to come up, alone, because that was what she'd asked. With his pistol ready? No — not yet. He wouldn't want any shooting . . . slam, slam, slam, went her heart. She was going to faint. She could feel the dark drumming vapour welling up . . . perhaps if she let them think she'd fainted . . . She slumped herself forward as far as the cords would let her, forcing her head down. The movement shifted the pillow-case a couple of inches, letting fresher air in. Faint but clear the whine of the lift-motor. Whispers from the men by the door. Silence. John's knock. Mrs Walsh's voice, dispassionate, totally under control.

"The door's open. Please come up."

John's steps climbing the bare treads, two at a time. Mrs Walsh again. "In there please."

Three more steps.

"Freeze! Hands on your head."

"I got the bugger . . ."

Then the explosion, stunning loud, right in the room. Louise's body leapt at the sound and this time she deliberately converted the movement into a lurch that unbalanced the chair completely. *If they start shooting, throw yourself flat.* The crash of her fall belted the breath out of her. It took her a moment to realise that not all the noise had been caused by her hitting the floor — there'd been another shot as she fell. The pillow-case was almost clear. She tried to thresh it away. No use. Her head still rang with the first explosion — perhaps it had had been one of those stun-bombs and not a shot. Through the ringing she heard new noises, grunts, thuds, threshings, gasps, the whole floor juddering with the movement. The fight rolled suddenly towards her. Something heavy and solid — a shod foot, she realised as the pain cleared — crashed against her forehead and swept by, taking the pillow-case with it. She could see.

She was lying on her side, looking slantwise across the room towards the corner between the windows and the door. The struggle was going on out of sight behind her head. Straight in front of her, face down on the bare boards, lay a man in blue paint-splashed overalls. His metal spectacles were twisted against his cheek. His cropped hair had been blond but was now a mess of blood. The back of his head was the wrong shape. Beyond the body Mrs Walsh sat slumped against the door-post. Her face was blue-white, her lips purple, moving as if she was muttering her prayers. A patch of blood was spreading across the grey wool of her suit, fresh glinting beadlets still seeping from the wound behind. Her toque lay upside-down against the skirting, the jewel hidden. As Louise watched she tried to reach for it, almost toppled, and then pulled herself into something like her proper erect posture. Her head came up and she noticed Louise. A last spark flashed into the death-dulling eyes.

"The blood of emperors," she announced, equal speaking to equal.

She reached again for the toque, fell with it just beyond her grasp, and lay still.

Feet on the stairs, running. A man in motor-bike leathers sprang into the room and crouched, his stubby gun at the ready. ZAP! said the scarlet letters on his chest. He held the pose for an instant and rushed out of Louise's line of sight, towards the fight. Instantly his place was taken by another man, also in leathers, also striking for a moment that same coiled-spring posture before rushing on. Louise glimpsed yellow lettering across his shoulders as he turned. Another shot filled the room, bringing back the momentary deafness. Before it cleared her eye was caught by a movement at the bottom of her field of vision. Legs going past the windows, workmen again, two of them, in an awkward scrambling run. The one in front carried a battered blue metal tool-case. As they went past the second window her chair was lifted bodily and set up-right. Hands began to work at her gag.

"Where's HRH?"

(John's voice, gasping and mumbled.)

"Here. Looks OK." (Close behind her.)

"Don't know about this one." (Third voice.) "That one looks a goner. What happened?"

"She got a gun somewhere and shot him in the back." (John.) "Gave me a chance to have a go at the other fucker."

"There. You OK, ma'am?"

The gag slid free. Louise spat vomit.

"Davy!" she croaked. "Other room!"

She twisted her head to see John and one of the men rush out. The other man was kneeling, cutting her loose. She was aware of the movements and voices of more men beyond the door. Calls from the hallway — "Not here!" "Here!"

She was free, but almost fell as she rose.

"Hold it, ma'am. Steady."

"No!"

She wrenched her arm free and ran to the lobby. It seemed full of police.

"Jesus!" called a voice. "Look at this!"

She pushed through. It was the room with the trunks in it, reeking of mothballs. The kitchen table was below the open window with a chair backed against it. Someone was already outside and John was on the table.

"That way!" she yelled. "Two of them! They've got him in a tool-case!"

John turned his head at her voice and did a thumbs-up sign. He scrambled through the window and another man climbed onto the table. She pushed through and shoved aside the man who was getting onto the chair.

"Wait! Hold it!" shouted someone.

"No!" she snapped. "I must!"

There was a moment's pause. (Later she realised that they must all have been waiting for one of the others to grab her, but none of them had the nerve.) In the half-second while she waited for the man to climb clear she glanced down. Almost straight below her, against the wall, was a tin trunk with its lid open. It was filled with a glittering white mass, like snow. Mothballs. Protruding from the snow, eyes staring up, was the face of a man. It was Alex Romanov. He was wearing some kind of reddy-black beret. The vision was sudden, hideous, intense enough to intrude for its instant into this other pounding nightmare Louise was in. She shook it away and climbed out into the open. Immediately her legs began running, dream-slow, that terrible inefficient female wallow, holding up the men behind her.

The others were at the corner. John rounded it and stopped. He pointed and yelled. The next man signalled violently to someone below. The man beyond was talking into an intercom.

"Gone down on the hoist!" John shouted. "Just the two of them. Boy's carrying a tool-case."

"Look there !" said a voice from behind Louise.

She turned. The men behind her were running the other way now. She followed, gasping, reached the other corner. There was another man with an intercom, listening and passing on what he heard in a steady, detached voice.

" . . . builder's truck, going towards visitors' car-park . . . "

Louise looked out over the parapet at the lawns and drives that led to the main gate. There was no traffic on the bridge. Several police cars, blue lights blinking, blocked the gateway. The tall iron gates were being pushed shut. Two ambulances came wailing up and stopped behind the police cars. A dozen policemen were shepherding sightseers across the lawns towards the south-west corner of the Palace. A green truck shot into sight from the archway to the visitors' car-park. It clearly came from the building-works, and had a couple of scaffold-planks lashed down from the cab roof to the tail-gate. Only its speed was out of context. The rear wheels slithered on the corner. The truck almost spun, but straightened and roared straight at the gates. Policemen leapt clear. It must have been doing well over thirty as it crashed into the iron-work, mounted a little way, slewed and stuck.

For a heartbeat no one did anything. The pain in Louise's throat told her she'd been screaming. The left-hand gate had lifted off its hinges under the impact and half fallen, with the nearside front wheel of the truck resting a little way up it. There was no movement from the cab, no sign. Men in combat gear emerged from behind the police cars, guns raised. A uniformed officer spoke through a loud hailer. Still nothing stirred by the truck. Covered by several guns a man approached it and tried the door-handle on the driver's side, but the door seemed to have jammed. Suddenly, as he wrenched, it opened and the head and shoulders of a man flopped out. The policeman caught the body deftly and dragged it clear, speaking over his shoulder as he did so. Another policeman approached the cab with his pistol raised. He spoke, but then stood back, still with the pistol poised to fire. Blue-trousered legs eased themselves off the seat as the passenger slid across and down. A boy, the policeman had said, surprisingly young to judge by his stature. He was wearing a blue denim cap. He had turned as he reached the ground to lift something from the cab, so Louise couldn't see his face, and then another half dozen police closed round and hid him completely.

"Better move back, ma'am," said one of the men beside Louise. "Looks like they've spotted you down there."

She glanced along the line of his gesture. The tourists were still being herded into the corner of the forecourt, but a number of them were taking their time, walking backwards with video cameras trained on the scene by the gate. Elsewhere in the gathering huddle Louise caught the familiar dark gleam of lenses trained on her. Automatically she moved out of shot to a point where she could still see between the crenellations what was happening round the truck.

One of the men there bent to pick something from the ground. His movement left a gap through which Louise could glimpse the prisoner for a moment. It wasn't a boy, it was a woman. Her cap had fallen off, letting her dark hair hang down. Louise still couldn't see her face as her head was bowed over the tool-case which she was now clutching with one arm against her chest. A man had gripped it by the handle and was trying to take it from her grasp. The first man rose, hiding her again, but in that couple of seconds Louise had recognised from the despairing and protective pose that the woman was Janine.

126

"I want to go home. I know I can't, but . . . "

"You've had a rougher time than you realise, darling."

"I'm all right. I was all right the moment Davy woke up and started yelling for his supper."

"They still don't know what he'd been given, or how much. They're expecting the lab reports around midnight."

"He's all right. I could hear it in the way he yelled. I just know. He's going to be black and blue, though they'd done the best they could about padding the tool-case and drilling air-holes. Will you make sure they let us have it in the end? I want to be able to show him one day. I don't like the idea of him not knowing."

"You're talking too much, darling. Take it easy."

"I want to talk. I want to know. Those other men — dressed like motor-bike couriers — where did they come from? How did they get there so fast?"

"I gather they were part of your escort. You'd told Inspector Yale you wanted just John and another car for this kind of visit. She consulted her superiors and they decided to over-rule you."

"Without telling me?"

"I'm afraid she turns out to have been right this time."

"Oh, hell . . . Where's my pad? Just make a note for me to thank her. . . . Have they told you anything about Janine?"

"I haven't seen her. So far all they know, at least all they're letting on, is that she was kidnapped this morning on her way to visit that aunt in Clapham. It's assumed they followed her there. They needed her to look after Davy. Once they'd got him, of course, they could make her do anything they wanted."

"I keep trying to think who knew I was going to see Aunt Bea today. I hadn't told anyone, practically — you, Father, Security, Aunt Bea — she'd have told Mrs Walsh, I suppose . . . "

"The idea at the moment seems to be that your attackers got themselves taken on at the building-works and used their access across the roofs to terrorise Mrs Walsh into co-operating with them."

"No."

"This would account for her sudden apparent change of heart about releasing your grandmother's papers, and also for the presence of poor Alex Romanov's body. He must have been there, attempting to negotiate with Mrs Walsh, when they first broke in, and they killed him to show her that they meant business."

"Nobody terrorised Mrs Walsh. It wasn't possible."

"Um."

"And all those mothballs!"

"Take it easy, darling."

"It's the worst thing, still. I don't know why. I keep seeing it when I close my eyes, over and over. Me up there on the table, waiting to get through the window, and then looking down and seeing him in the trunk with his head sticking out of this white stuff. Everything else I could understand — it was bad, frightful, but I understood it. That was just pure ghastly. Meaningless. Like tearing a scab off the world and seeing what's underneath is madness."

"Try not to think about it."

"I want to talk to Janine. With no one listening."

"I'll see what can be done."

JUNE 1988

I

The Garden Party was Soppy's first official public appearance since coming out of the clinic. Louise caught only occasional glimpses of her. The form for Garden Parties, assuming tolerable weather, was that the guests trooped through to the lawns and assembled, just over a thousand of them, and stood around for a while, half-listening to the band, chatting to chance-met friends, criticising the colour-clashes in the formal bedding — Mother, after years of careful diplomacy, had realised at last that the only choice she had was between sacking Mr Farren or going along with him — until the Family emerged, separated and began to move through the crowd. Piers, on the couple of occasions he'd come, had claimed to be fascinated by the dynamics of this process. The guests were a random mass, culled from the length and breadth of Britain for disparate reasons, social, charitable, political, inexplicable. They had no joint will but only, most of them, the individual hope of being presented to a member of the Family and exchanging a banal sentence or two. But they behaved as though it was a game with definite rules which they all almost at once understood and obeyed.

As Louise progressed across the grass a pathway opened before her, about a yard wide, lined by guests waiting for their chance of a greeting. The pathway stretched only a few paces ahead but it was always there, stopping when she stopped to talk and wriggling on another couple of yards as she moved on again. Sometimes, just as randomly, it forked and a decision had to be made, the unused path closing as soon as it became clear that she was going to take the other one. Louise's lady-in-waiting and equerry moved with her, usually a pace behind, but edging ahead when they had spotted one of the faces on their lists so that they could be ready to present the selected citizen to her. One trap was that everybody in the crowd knew who you were and looked at you with the natural gleam of recognition to which you instinctively felt urged to respond. According to Piers there was a specialised bit of brain which did nothing but remember faces; he said Louise's must be hyperdeveloped, but even so she was sometimes tricked by the response-instinct. Usually, though, she could rely on herself to pick out some anxious smiler, nod, give the brain a half-second to do its trick, and then say, "Hello, Matron. I'm so glad you could come because I've been longing to know how that baby got on, the little Asian girl you were fitting for a new foot." It was a bit of an ego-trip, to be honest, the ability to do that after an eight-month gap and see the pleasure on the woman's face and feel the ripple of approval round her. The others could do it too — it was part of the job — but Louise seemed to have inherited Mother's natural knack whereas Albert, like Father, had had to train himself.

There were moments when two paths crossed. You would smile at Albert or whoever but then turn and talk to a guest while your attendants, with glances and minimal gestures, would organise separating paths to carry the royal wanderers apart. Like particles colliding in a cloud-chamber, Piers said. Louise glimpsed Soppy at two or three such encounters, looking perfectly stunning, everyone's dream princess, in a wide-brimmed black hat and bell-skirted electric-blue dress with a high collar. She was still bung full of drugs but looked the picture of health, smiling and pink, but not saying much to anyone beyond "hello". She had a slight stammer these days, even alone, with people she knew well. Albert was extremely protective of her and insisted she was getting better.

After the wandering-through-crowd process you sat down to tea at your unofficially official table and chosen guests were brought to sit with you for a few minutes each. These might be anyone from people you yourself had asked to see to the unlucky daughters of skilled mums who'd managed to importune your equerry. Even meeting these last might not be pointless. For instance, at the previous Garden Party Louise had found a girl who had done a stint in the field with Wells for the Sahel and had learnt that the Director she had thought so unspeakable at that City luncheon was extremely popular with his staff. This afternoon she got a different sort of view from the underside — a student from Piers's university, reading Spanish but deep into student politics and full of good gossip to tell Piers.

As the sitting-down episode ended you did a quick check with your minders to see if anyone who mattered had been missed and then there was another half hour of crowd-wandering, different because the guests tended to have separated into clumps, and then Mr Slocombe would ring a hand-bell and bellow for everyone to be upstanding and the band would play "God Save the King". The Family would re-form as a unit, move off to the doors of the Yellow Drawing-room, turn on the step, wave, wait for the muttered, under-stated cheer, barely audible against the burr of traffic up Buckingham Palace Road, and vanish into the temporary and partial privacy of the Blue Boudoir for a stiff drink. Ladies-in-waiting and equerries would arrive a few minutes later, peering at semi-decipherable notes they had scribbled about the various royal encounters. Father's idea was that it saved time in the long run if you sorted out anything quick and easy while it was still in the top drawer of memory.

Louise saw Albert massaging the knuckles of the hand Soppy had been holding, his eyes on the door. She raised her eyebrows into a query. He made a thumbs-up. When Soppy came in she stood at the door and checked where he was but then, with a visible mild effort, looked round the rest of the room and came across to Louise.

"No Piers?"

"Working. How are you? You look terrific."

"Better, they keep telling me. Bloody drugs bung my guts up, so they give me a foul pink powder to open them out, but I'm never sure when. How's Davy d-doing?"

"Fine, only he's bolshie about crawling. He prefers to shove himself around on his bum."

"Like a dog with worms. Going to have another one?"

"I thought I'd try and aim for August, when there's more

room in the diaries. That's what I did last time, but of course I missed."

"I want to, and my trick-cyclist says it might help. Kill or cure. Do you think it'd be f-fair on the brat? With a mum like me? Tell me the truth, darling. Nothing else is any use."

It wasn't an easy question. Even before her breakdown Soppy had seemed an oddly brusque and casual mother. Both kids were rather quiet and cautious, though not to an extent you could call disturbed. According to Albert they had minded the sudden sacking of their nanny last autumn much more than Soppy's absence in hospital.

"I suppose it depends," said Louise. "If you want it just to help you get well, then I don't think it is fair. If you want it so that it can be itself, for its own sake, then it is."

"Won't find that out till I've had it. No, thanks."

The last two words were spoken to a maid who'd come by with a tray of chipolatas.

"I don't believe it," said Louise.

"Only at meals. Point is, I've got to show 'em I can. Show myself too. When I came out of the nut-house I got a lock put on the fridges and gave Mrs Alphege the key, but it was a bit like wearing a chastity belt, so I said don't bother. I allow myself third helpings on Sundays."

"I saw you playing polo on the box."

"Could have been worse. More hacks than spectators and I played like a dead haddock for the first couple of chukkas, but then I got my eye in and started hitting the odd ball. I'm getting on pretty well with Bertie these days, you know. I really need him. Him and no one else."

"I noticed you looking a bit lovey-dovey."

"Only I wish people wouldn't keep forgiving me the whole time."

"There isn't much to forgive."

"Wish I thought so. Don't go. Something I wanted to ask you."

The various teams were coming in, but Soppy had gripped Louise by the wrist. Her fingers were like steel.

"It's about forgiving. That nurse of yours — Bert says you wanted to have her back."

"Not really. Well, I mean, yes, part of me wanted to try

and pretend that none of that had ever happened. She was so exactly my idea of what a nanny should be — only she wasn't. Another part of me was furious with her, and terrified about what might have happened. Now I'm just mainly sorry for her, and the mess she's in."

"They going to put her in prison?"

"Well, she'll have to be tried. The trouble is that her best defence is going to be telling the court what really happened . . ."

"*That's* what I want to know. I've got a sort of feeling for her. I mean we both landed everyone in the shit just about the same time. She wasn't off her trolley, like me though, was she?"

"No. She was just trying to be loyal in too many directions at once. It's like whoever-it-was said about Northern Ireland — there wasn't enough loyalty to go round. She'd grown up as an only. Her parents ran a corner-shop in Ormskirk, too busy to have much time for her. She used to play with a kid across the street, a boy called Ian. He was bright, got scholarships, finished up on some kind of exchange at Bremen University, fell in with one of those crazy anarchist cells and got hooked. He told Janine all about it — they used to meet up still whenever they got the chance, in fact they were just like brother and sister, only he didn't show up on her vetting. We don't know how he linked in with the Gorman lot — there aren't supposed to be that many connections between the Red Brigades and the Irish thugs. One theory is that he actually went and made the approach himself when Janine got her job. Anyway, he turned up in London and suggested a meeting on her day out, which was perfectly natural, but then he started being a bit too inquisitive about her job, which wasn't — before he'd always taken the line that we were an obscene farce. When she challenged him he told her that there were some political prisoners he wanted to help, and he was hoping she could tell him some kind of state secret he could use to bargain with. She said she wasn't interested, and changed the subject. He made her promise to say nothing about it, which she did. But the next time he rang she told him she'd worked out that the political prisoners he'd been talking about had been the Chester bombers and she was going to tell Security. He said that if she did that Gorman would have him killed for talking to her without their permission, and quite likely her too. He managed to frighten her enough to make her keep quiet a little longer."

"He was ringing her at Quercy, through your exchange?"

"No. She had an aunt in Clapham she used to visit on her day off. She'd given him that number. Next time he called he managed to persuade her that if she helped him to discover some kind of family secret he could use it wouldn't only remove the threat to his life and hers, it would also mean the Family itself wouldn't be so much of a target. I'm not sure she really believed him — she says she did — they'd had a relationship of total trust so far, she thought — but I think she was just stringing him along and hoping that if she didn't do anything the whole problem would go away. There wasn't that much chance of her finding anything useful in any case. But just so as she could have the odd titbit to keep him happy with she'd started listening to Piers and me having our goodnight chats. We always do. It helps me go to sleep. We've got a fancy kind of baby-alarm — a friend of Piers invented it — it does all sorts of extra tricks you never really need. Anyway, that's how she learnt about Granny's letters, and Aunt Bea having all the papers at Hampton Court, and so on. Ian had managed to persuade her, she says, that he wasn't interested in violence either, and he pretended to get very excited about the papers, but of course all he really wanted to know was when was I going to visit Aunt Bea, and if possible when I'd be taking Davy with me. Then when you did your bolt things got urgent, both sides, but by then they'd got themselves jobs on the Hampton Court site, and sussed the flats out, and all they had to do was pick Janine up on her way to the Clapham aunt . . . I wish you'd seen the way she was holding Davy when she got out of the truck. She'd got a broken arm too. You'd know why I can't help wanting to have her back . . ."

"Poor kid. Poor stupid kid. People keep trying to tell me it wasn't my fault, coming apart like that. But Piers is wrong, you know. There was always a real me somewhere. I'm just as much to blame as your girl."

"Nonsense. You weren't breaking any laws, for a start."

"Doesn't make any difference. Love to old Piers, darling. Wish I'd have taken his line from the start."

Soppy smiled like the happiest person in the world and turned away. They'd never have let her, thought Louise. Piers can, because he's a man, but princesses are there for the public to screw in their dreams. She watched Soppy sidle her way through the now crowded room towards Albert. Louise had done most of her sorting-out at the tea-table, so was finished before the others. Sir Savile noticed her standing alone and came over.

"You laid on a decent day for us this time, Sir Sam."

"Thank you, ma'am. We endeavour to give satisfaction."

"That sounds like the punch-line to one of Uncle Ted's stories."

"It used to be what the bishop said to the actress. I have no idea who the participants might be these days. Ahem. Something a little unforeseen has occurred, in which I thought you might be interested. You remember that upleasant business with the Dowager Princess's papers?"

"What do you mean remember?"

"We have received a letter from a woman, claiming to be Mrs Walsh's daughter."

"She can't be. The daughter was Down's syndrome, or something of that kind."

"The letter is from a professional scribe in Dushanbe."

"Where's that?"

"Capital of Tadzhikstan, apparently. Southern USSR — right down beyond Tashkent."

"Oh, yes, of course!"

Sir Savile raised an eyebrow and waited.

"Go on," said Louise. "What does the letter say?"

"It is in English of a sort, and sufficiently peculiar not to appear simply a hoax or confidence trick. Apparently Mrs Walsh paid the woman an allowance, which has naturally now ceased to arrive. She wants HM to put that right. There is an implication that failing satisfaction she has secrets of some kind to reveal. She believes that we can arrange for her to be given travel documents so that she can come and talk to HM. There was no estate, I think, apart from a piece of jewellery."

"One whopping diamond brooch and a Fabergé egg to keep it in. They must be worth a quid or two between them. She told me she'd burnt everything else or chucked it in the river. Any chance you can get this woman over? I'd really love to talk to her. I'd pay the air fare."

"I could put in a word at the consular department, but perhaps . . ."

"Hold it. How far is Dushanbe from Baku?"

"Several hundred miles, I should think. Getting on a thousand."

"Piers has got a conference in September — you've got it in the schedules. I've decided I'm going with him, whatever anyone says. I've made a five-day hole in my diaries."

Louise knew Sir Savile well enough to be aware of the sudden discomfort under the permanent light tan.

"It's really a matter between HM and HMG," he said. "Are you aware that there is already a question of HM visiting Moscow next year? HMG are going to advise against it on the grounds that the Russian government have not yet acknowledged their guilt in the murder of the late Tsar and his family."

"But really because Mrs T. wants to screw them a bit more over human rights. You leave Mrs T. to me, Sir Sam. I dropped a couple of hints when I met her at that anti-litter beano. I think she'd quite like to let me go, partly because it'd be one in the eye for the FO, and partly to show everyone that not letting Father go really is a matter of principle, because he's head of state. So I want you to deal with your pals at the FO for me. They haven't got any real reasons — it's just they want a quiet life. So you can tell them that if they make trouble not only will they have Mrs T. putting the boot in from the other side, but I'll leak it to the hacks who stopped me."

This time anyone could have read Sir Savile's expression. Louise had just broken a whole chapter in the *Manual of Unwritten Rules*.

"I'm serious," she said. "If it's any help you can tell them it'll be a private visit but I'm prepared to wave the flag for them a couple of times . . . hey, that might work . . . see if they can't lay on something for me down that way . . . Oh, don't look so bothered — I promise you they'll cave in as soon as you let them see we mean it."

He managed not to sigh. Albert was right, she thought — time he went.

"May I suggest, ma'am, that before we book the flight for you we attempt to check whether the woman is who she claims to be."

"Oh, she's pukka. Even if she isn't Down's syndrome, she's pukka."

2

"Let's hope so. Dad keeps saying it's treatable, but that might mean anything. I just can't see her going back to where she started."

"You wouldn't want her to, surely. That would be the context she was in when she bolted off to Argentina."

"I didn't mean that. I meant before. When everything was all right."

"Seemed to be all right, but already presumably containing the seeds of the breakdown. Her only hope is to go on from there."

"Yes, of course, only . . . I suppose what I'm saying is I just feel where she's at now won't work. It's over the top still. Even something I ought to be happy about, like her being so lovey-dovey with Bert. I feel it just can't last. It's another kind of bolting . . . Did I tell you about poor old Sir Sam thinking I'm about to do a bolt too?"

"Uh?"

"I broke it to him I'm coming with you to Baku."

"How did he take it?"

"I didn't give him a chance to think about it. I told him I was going on from there to Dushanbe to meet Mrs Walsh's daughter. Father's had a letter from her asking why the money's stopped coming Mrs Walsh used to pay her. I looked Dushanbe up on the map. It's about two hundred miles south of Tashkent, right up in the mountains, almost into India. She must have been born up there, somewhere."

"How far is Dushanbe from Baku?"

"A bit over a thousand miles, I think. I'll have to fix for them to let me open a trade fair or something."

"You are proposing to sell Stilton and Paisley shawls to the inhabitants of the High Pamir?"

"I thought I might get them to bring her a bit of the way to meet me. It doesn't have to be an actual trade fair. Tashkent's quite a big place, I think."

"It still seems to me that you are asking people to make very considerable concessions to satisfy a minor interest of yours."

"I think you're being bloody unsupportive. I am absolutely determined to meet Rose Walsh somehow or other. It's my turn to make a nuisance of myself, anyway. I'm tired of being everybody's goody goody all the time. Besides, I've always wanted to go to Tashkent."

SEPTEMBER 1988

I

Standing on the dam, staring out at the enormous dun land-scape, Louise recognised what she saw — a major ecological cock-up. She had seen the same thing before, in and around the Sahel, some grandiose scheme, billions of money, years of planning and labour, villages and tribes forcibly resettled, centuries-old ways of life wiped away, and nothing at the end but a useless dam on the edge of a new-made desert (nothing, that is, apart from spectacular up-wellings of cash thousands of miles away in a number of Swiss bank accounts).

She kept smiling, kept asking the questions that wouldn't embarrass. So this was Tashkent. The name had seemed pure romance, but so far the visit had consisted of officials and the wives of officials, more nervous even than those of home counties aldermen. There had been a motorcade along streets of cheap modern blocks, tattily flagged for the occasion. There had been a mosque converted to a museum, but none of the private houses converted to mosques, mentioned in Louise's FO briefing. There had been parades of pretty and well-drilled children with dances to do and flags to wave and songs of unity and friendship to sing. There had been a walkabout through narrow-laned quarters refurbished and re-Asiaticised (Louise's translator actually used the word) over the past few years to attract tourists, but today scoured clean of tourists and peopled with folk-costumed locals for her to walk about among — real people, these, under the fancy dress, grinning welcome, knowing who she was, exuding extraordinary waves of happiness that she should be there, as though her presence had an unknowable talismanic meaning for them. Of course to balance that plus there'd been the hacks, both Russian and imported, jostling and importuning, but mostly held at bay by phalanxes of security men, rougher and more obtrusive than the ones she was used to. By the end of the walkabout the conflict had become ugly. Louise kept smiling, kept looking the other way, but at the last stall she stopped and bought a pretty beaded handbag as a present for Inspector Yale.

Then there had been the luncheon, endless with its speeches and toasts. And now this desert. Somewhere out beyond it were other deserts across which armies had conquered and fled, lakes and mountain ranges, vast dead cities, tombs of dynasties, sand-swallowed castles, a history older than Europe's, none of which she was going to see but instead had to stand and smile at this boring and disastrous dam. Still, she could feel those other places and the peoples to whom they were home. Despite the drab western suits of the officials she was aware of being in a context every bit as alien as Africa.

They were an hour and a half behind schedule — better than he'd expected, according to the cat-faced second secretary sent down from the Moscow embassy to help shepherd her around. It was late afternoon before the motorcade swished once more through the dreary suburbs, and dusk when at last she was settled into a courtyard near the heart of the city. There was a dry fountain, five dusty trees, iron tables and chairs fresh-painted in her honour, catenaries of coloured light-bulbs under the branches. Waiters brought beakers of delicious cold lemon sherbet flavoured with unfamiliar herbs, and flat mustardy biscuits to nibble. A space had been left vacant across the table from Louise, but no chair. After a short while a woman was led up and stood there, waiting.

Louise was angry. She had expressly asked to see Mrs Walsh's daughter alone, and had been told it would be arranged. She turned and smiled at the secretary of the local Party, and saw from his answering twitch of a smile that he was unsure of his ground.

"I'd like to talk to her in private," she said. "I thought we'd got all that fixed. It's been such a good visit — it'd be a pity to spoil it."

Carrie rose. The man from the Moscow embassy followed

her lead. Louise kept her smile and her stare fixed on the secretary until the nasty little crook gave in, nodded, muttered to his gang and led them away. Louise turned to the woman.

They'd probably fetched her from the mountains days ago and now kept her hanging around since dawn, but you couldn't tell. She had that look of someone who could wait for years, patient as a rock on a hillside. The patience wasn't humble or cowering. She returned Louise's look directly, as if entirely immune to the mystic rays of royalty which made almost everyone else Louise met so jumpy. She was wearing a heavy black dress and a black shawl wrapped round her head and under her chin. She was indistinguishable from the dozens of local women Louise had seen that day. She wasn't the snub-nosed Tartar Louise had imagined, but had a bony, beaky face, black eyes deep set, and a weathered, yellow-olive skin. Probably with the flatter features of a baby she had looked more nearly Mongoloid.

"Hullo, Rose," said Louise. "I'm so glad you could come. Do sit down."

"Ullo, ducks," said Rose, at the same time spreading her skirt and doing a perfectly controlled curtsey.

"Please sit down," said Louise again. "I hope you haven't forgotten your English after all these years."

"Yes. Been years," said Rose.

She sat and waited.

"I thought you'd like me to tell you how your mother died," said Louise. "And I was hoping you'd tell me something of what you know about her, and your father, and anything else you can remember."

"Ah, she was a bad 'un," said Rose.

Louise smiled encouragingly, but Rose hesitated and then asked what was clearly a question in a foreign language.

"I'm afraid not," said Louise. "Is that Iranian?"

"Tadzhiki Irani," said Rose hopefully.

Louise glanced across the courtyard. The interpreter was sitting with the officials, all of them pretending not to look in her direction. The interpreter had spoken both Russian and Iranian, but had flattened things out, making them nuanceless, lifeless. He had slowed everything down, too. There wasn't that much time now, after the long delays.

"Let's see how we get on," she said. "I'm sure it will come back."

"Never learned me, my mum," said Rose.

She paused, assembling forgotten words. Louise smiled, understanding.

"Irani she learned me . . . Fred, he'd of learned me . . . He was that scared . . . They learned me a bit at the home . . . clean them toilets, Maria . . . scrub them steps . . . only when I come to the works . . . got talking with a few mates . . . found I wasn't a loony . . . learned a bit off my mates . . . not much cop."

"I think you're doing very well. There's so much I want to know. Fred? Was that your father?"

Rose shook her head.

"Khan Kalun, my dad was. Back here. Mum made out as it was Fred."

"Yes, I see. Then how did you get out here? How did you find your way? Did she send you, in the end?"

"Not her. Didn't want to know me. It was the Party done it. Had this strike, see. I was in it. Looking for workers been done wrong, they was, so I told them, see? Put me on to Mr Grindle."

"He was a lawyer? A solicitor?"

"Right. Got me out of the home. But he couldn't find Fred. Lot of blokes called Walsh, he says. But there was this march, see. Up in London, it was, into this park place. Knew it at once, I did. Gone off and looked for the house. Copper won't let me by, see. But I tells Mr Grindle and he tries again. Nother bloody big house, nother copper won't let me by. This man comes up, he's old, walking with a stick, see. 'That's him,' says the copper. 'Fred,' I says. Cor, did he jump? He was that scared. Sat in this garden, we did. 'Go away,' he says. 'Go away or she'll do us. Back of the head, like she done the others. Go to Ura Tyube where you belong'. Wrote it down, he did. Got it here."

She reached in among the folds of her dress and took out a small soft leather wallet from which, carefully, she removed a rectangular object and passed it across. It turned out to be a flattened cigarette pack, Capstan. Just readable on the creased and softened cardboard was a line of pencil writing in shaky, sloping capitals. Louise handed it back.

"Mr Grindle, he fixed about the money with my mum," said Rose.

"And then you just came out here, like that?" said Louise. Maria shrugged.

"There was the camps, a-course. Dunno how long. Years. I come when they let us go. Took a bit of asking. Then someone says about this khan, got himself shot by this foreign woman what he found. Back of his head, just like Fred said. Run off with the other bloke. Didn't want to know me, first off. Wrote to Mr Grindle and he started sending the money. After that it was all right. Got a lot of nevvies now. Nevvies and . . . and . . . "

"Nieces?"

"Right."

There was a pause.

"Do you want to know what happened to your mother?" said Louise.

"She's dead. Made her pay for what she done to me, didn't I? Done to me and Fred? Right up to the end I made her pay. Ah, she was a bad un."

"Yes, I think so too. But she saved my son's life, I think, just before she died. Shall I tell you about it?"

Rose shrugged again. The officials were watching now, beginning to move restlessly on their chairs. No wonder, if Rose had been in the camps, there had been such obstacles to this meeting. Louise explained as simply as she could what had happened that day at Hampton Court. She wasn't sure how much Rose understood.

"I still don't know why she did it," she said. "She may have been madder than I realised. She had made her life the way she chose, and she wasn't going to let anyone change it, not even terrorists with guns."

"Only thing she knows. You're in her way. Bang. Shot Fred, did she?"

"Oh, I don't think so. He was a good deal older than she was. I imagine he just died of natural causes. Look, I brought this for you."

The officials had risen and were moving towards them as

143

Louise took the old blue box from her bag and passed it across. Rose pressed the catch and gazed, nodding, apparently unastonished. She lifted the jewelled egg from its velvet nest and turned it over.

"Ah," she said, in a tone of recognition.

It had taken Louise twenty minutes to find the secret catch — you twisted the head of an agate leopard — but Rose seemed to know what she was looking for. The egg separated into its two halves, joined at the hinge. By now the officials had reached the table and crowded round, craning as Rose lifted the brooch out and held it up. The coloured lights of the courtyard were caught and reflected by the facets. One of the officials spoke.

"Is it genuine? he asks," said the interpreter.

"Yes," said Louise. "It belongs to Rose here. It was her mother's."

She was not at all certain about this — there was a strong probability, she thought, that Mrs Walsh had stolen it with the rest of the jewels after the last of the Belayevs had died on their terrible journey. In that case it would probably belong to the state, and finish up unbecomingly on the bosom of the local secretary's wife. She was determined to hand the jewel over as publicly as possible, to make sure that didn't happen.

"'Sright," said Rose. "My mum's that was. Got it from her mum — some nob give it her."

"How did you know?" said Louise.

"Me uncle, he tells me. Dead now. Always on about that there egg. Me dad took it off her. Her wossname? When a girl gets married, see?"

"Dowry, you mean?" said Louise.

"Dowry," said Rose. "'Sright. Then my mum run off with it when she done my dad in, see?"

"I had it valued," said Louise. "It's a very good stone, but the egg is probably worth as much. It isn't Fabergé's own work, but it does come from his workshop. I've often wondered why your mother didn't sell it and make herself more comfortable. Anyway, it's yours now."

Rose put the jewel back into its nest, closed the egg and laid it back in the box, which she shut and pushed back across the table.

"Ta, but no," she said.

"You could sell it," said Louise. "Build yourself a nice house — or use some of it to help with your nieces' dowries."

"Dowries are no longer permitted," said the interpreter in the deadpan voice of one announcing the official line regardless of its relationship to facts.

"She was a bad un," said Rose. "Made her pay, long as she lived, I did. Wasn't for the money. It was for what she done to people. Don't want nothing from her now. She was a bad un."

She pushed the box emphatically towards Louise.

"You have it," she said. "Won't look daft, you wearing something like that. You're the sort."

Louise shook her head. The protocol of gifts to royalty was far too complex to explain now.

"I'm afraid I'm not allowed to take presents from people," she said. "It's against the rules."

"Give it someone else, then," said Rose.

Now that the leather box was closed the almost magical power the jewel had exerted was lost. Louise could sense the anxiety and impatience of the officials. Carrie did her double cough, the signal that the schedule demanded a move. Louise took the box and stood up. Rose stood up too.

"Tell you what," said Louise. "I'll look after it for the time being, but it's still yours. When I get home I'll get a lawyer to draw out a deed of gift — that'll take a month or two, so you'll have time to change your mind. I'll make the deed to a charity called Wells for the Sahel. It's a very good cause. They can sell this and use the money. That way it'll save a lot of children from dying of starvation. OK?"

(Seventy new wells, about — or two years' salary and expenses for the Director.)

"OK," said Rose, smiling for the first time — her mother's thin-lipped smile, but in Rose wholly different. It was true all through her, Louise realised, the sameness and the difference, the force of will, the singleness of aim, the immediate sense of grandeur you felt on meeting her, and the other sense, more slowly realised, that she had created herself and her world to be what she chose, unaided. The difference lay in the nature of that choice.

145

Rose shook hands, and did her curtsey. Fred must have taught her that, Louise thought. Then she turned away and was hidden as the dismal officials closed round the table.

2

The conference had almost been cancelled at the last minute, because of the growing ethnic unrest, and the marches and demonstrations on the streets of Baku. One of the organising committee had told Piers that it was Louise who had saved it. Somebody in the Kremlin had decided that the royal presence might be a help, by distracting the world media for a few days, so the venue had been switched to a holiday complex forty miles up the coast. That had sounded idyllic, but when they got there they found that they were looking out over the results of another ecological cock-up but on an immensely grander scale than anything Louise had seen before. Thanks to irrigation schemes and uncontrolled pollution along the Volga, the Caspian had shrunk. Beneath the hotel windows the great pale lake was dying. The exposed shoreline stank, despite attempts to spray it with deodorants. But how could you be sure, said Piers, that exactly the same thing wouldn't have happened if there had still been Tsars?

Louise reached the hotel just before two in the morning. The lights were on in the living-room of the suite, and the floor around the ludicrously ornate sofa was strewn with scribbled foolscap sheets. The air smelt as though Piers had spent the evening experimenting with joss-sticks. The bedroom door was open, with a low light shining beyond. Louise went quietly through, expecting to find Piers asleep, but he was sitting on the far edge of the bed rubbing his eczema cream into his shins. The relaxed curve of his spine and the repetitive self-hypnotising motion told her that he was still deep in the invisible maze of his work, lost, happy, infinities of thought beyond her reach; but when she passed the edge of his vision on her way to the bathroom he looked up.

"Back, darling? What's the time?"
"Getting on two. You've had a good day."

"How did you know? Excellent."

"What on earth have you been burning through there?"

"Joe Matalamaya's cheroots. The chap you danced with."
Louise laughed at the memory. Professor Matalamaya
was about fifty, bald, short, tubby, with a reddish copper
skin and an equally metallic accent — Philippine crossed with
Chicago, someone had told her. For five minutes he had
made her believe she could really waltz.

"It turns out he and I have been spending the last eighteen
months solving each other's problems," said Piers. "I've read
his papers of course and he's read mine, but you tend not to
publish accounts of the brick walls you've been banging your
head against."

"So it was worth coming?"

"Was it not! I'll try and explain if you like."

"Let me do my teeth. Did you remember to ring home in
the excitement?"

"He's starting a cold. That tooth's right through. Helen
got him to burble at me but I don't know how to pass that
on."

As they lay in the dark Louise could feel Piers's happiness like
a soft current flowing into her, easing the exhaustions and
disappointments of what had been a twenty-hour day. It
struck her that it was a long time since she had felt quite like
this about him, as though they were the only two people in
the universe, and all life, everything that mattered, existed in
the mysterious field of attraction between their poles. Then,
from the moment she had had her first scan, seen the
shadowy shape of Davy beginning to grow into existence,
felt him shrug himself to a new position in her womb, there
had been a third pole in the field, distorting the simplicities of
the original pattern, twisting the currents along new lines. A
life, a treasure, had been gained, but something had been lost.
Tonight she felt as if she had been given it back. It didn't
matter that she was too tired to make love — Piers wouldn't
want to anyway, not in this mood . . . She sensed a slight
change in him, the vaguest disruption in his purring content.

"You don't have to," she said. "I wouldn't understand,
would I, however easy you made it?"

"You don't mind?"

"No. In fact I rather like it like that, I think. I mean knowing there's something out there, different, right beyond my reach, something I can't touch or change or make what I want it to be. Pure."

"It's a point of view."

"You can't either, can you? I mean you can get out there somehow and find it and explore it, but you can't change it. You can't ever make it into something it isn't."

"What prompts these lucubrations?"

"I don't know. Meeting Rose, I suppose. Mrs Walsh's daughter."

"Pukka?"

"Absolutely. Don't you want to go on thinking?"

"Much better not. I'm on a sort of abstract high. I need a few concrete particularities to slow me down. Tell me about Rose."

Louise told him. The flight back from Tashkent had taken almost four hours. She'd had plenty of time to sort the events through in her own mind, and make guesses about what they meant, but for the moment she stuck to plain narrative. It didn't take long.

"She kept calling the man Fred?" said Piers. "Wasn't his name John?"

"Colonel John Walsh. That's the name on the book."

"Could have been John Frederick. Or like old Professor Onions, who everyone called Pete except his wife."

"You didn't read the book. Do you remember I told you about the fight by the railway-siding, when Mrs Walsh first met him? There was another Englishman, who got shot. 'My servant, poor Fred Creech.'"

"I suppose it's a possibility. The question is whether it's a necessary hypothesis."

"How am I supposed to tell?"

"The current orthodoxy is that you grade hypotheses according to their explanatory power. That in turn depends on what you wish to explain."

"I want to know what happened. Three lots of what happened, I suppose. What happened in the real adventure? What happened to Maria? What happened to Alex?"

"Alex? I thought Gorman shot him. He'd had the bad luck to come round and see Mrs Walsh while Gorman was setting things up, didn't he?"

"She was buying mothballs before that. She wanted to stop the body smelling. She'd shot other people in the back of the head, according to Fred. She'd got a gun, the one she shot Gorman with. It was part of Colonel Walsh's uniform. I think she kept it in a funny lacquered table she had on the landing."

"And she shot him out of habit? He was being a nuisance about your grandmother's papers so she asked him round and put a bullet in him? Your hypothesis begins to falter, darling."

"No. It wasn't like that. I'm almost sure. We'd all been working ourselves into a stew about Granny's papers getting out. That's all we could think of. But I don't believe that was what was worrying Mrs Walsh at all. Suppose when Great-grandfather was still alive somebody'd found out Colonel Walsh wasn't Colonel Walsh at all, but only poor old Fred Creech, an ex-servant, pulling a fast one — the Walshes would have been out on their ears, wouldn't they? Even after that, when he'd retired and they were living at Hampton Court — I mean if they'd got there by false pretences in the first place . . . I think what Mrs Walsh was really scared about was something she'd found in one of *Alex's* letters. He was the one who passed on the *émigré* gossip, remember. It might have been something his mother had told him ages ago, when he was still a boy, and he'd passed on and then forgotten about. Or perhaps I reminded him that evening he came to supper, and he got so frustrated with Mrs Walsh that he tried to use it to twist her arm . . . "

"All right. That will do as a possibility. It certainly seems a stronger motive for Mrs Walsh's behaviour than fear of exposure of their original book as fraudulent. That has never seemed to me fully plausible."

"I'll tell you something funny. From the moment Mrs Walsh first mentioned her baby I knew it mattered. I suppose it was because of me having just had Davy. I'm glad I met Rose, only there's such a lot I don't know still. She's just like her mother in some ways. Extraordinary will-power. Force of character. The difference is, she's good."

"You can tell?"

149

"Oh, yes. In my work, you know. I don't think you can tell straight off if someone's bad, and anyway most people are sort of in-between, but from time to time I meet — oh, for instance, that surgeon at the blind children's institute at Entebbe, remember? Lucy Ndolo? — people like that. You know. You feel it. I've seen a whole group of hacks suddenly realise what they've got in front of them and be pretty well bowled over — Rose's one of them. Given different chances in life she could have been as famous as Mother Teresa. As it is she does it for what she calls her nephews and nieces. And just think of her being wheeled round Hyde Park by a frightened, tipsy little man who was the only person in her childhood who gave her anything like love!"

"Under an assumed name."

"That's the point. He loved her because he could be himself with her. Fred Creech. He wasn't allowed to teach her English, but he taught her how to curtsey. Mrs Walsh talked to her in Iranian — that's what the Tadzhiks speak — but only a few words, for orders. When they got to India, you see, Rose was just a tiny baby, and it didn't matter her looking a bit foreign. But as soon as she started losing that baby face people could see there was something odd. They'd used her as part of their act — Mother, father, baby, escaped from the Reds after terrible adventures — and now she was beginning to look as though she couldn't be *their* baby, and perhaps they weren't pukka either . . . So Mrs Walsh's answer was to say she was Down's syndrome. Mongol, they'd have called it then. Not letting her speak English was part of that. And when she couldn't keep that up any longer she put her in a home. I'm fairly sure about all that, though I still think it's amazing she got away with it."

"People accept what they're told they're perceiving. There's been a lot of work done on it."

"I don't know what happened next. There was this strike at the factory, she said, and the Party took her on and showed she wasn't a loony and got her out of the home. That's how I know about the home. She must have been pretty well grown up by then if she was working in a factory, and surely people must have realised she wasn't MSN before that."

"They might have realised but not let on. I spent my

childhood in places like that, remember. I was comparatively lucky, but even with us there were staff who'd come there as kids and been kept on for the mucky jobs. Some were a bit retarded. They didn't get paid much — worked for their keep."

"Yes. I can see Mrs Walsh putting her daughter somewhere like that. There'd be an understanding. Provided she wasn't bothered she wouldn't ask any questions. But how did Rose ever get out?"

"Called up for war-work?"

"Oh, yes, of course. Then some kind of strike led by the Communists. She must have gone to them with her problem. She's not very articulate, in English, anyway."

"Learnt it late, from work-mates. The Party might have taken her on as a sort of mascot."

"She was on some kind of demo up in London when she recognised Hyde Park and wandered around and found KP. Security wouldn't let her through of course, but that gave her a line and she found the Walshes. Fred, anyway. He said what I told you. Next thing I know she's out here, in the camps."

"The Party could have helped her get a visa and so on, but those days she would have been arrested pretty well as soon as she'd stepped off the boat."

"I think her lawyer had come to some kind of an arrangement with Mrs Walsh to pay her an allowance provided she went back to Russia and stayed there. When she'd got out of the camps she somehow made her way down to Tadzhikstan — a place called Dzhalal Abad which Fred had told her about, and asked around until she heard a story about some petty khan, years before, whose people had found two strangers dying of hunger. He'd taken them into his camp and kept the woman as one of his wives, but one night she'd taken his pistol and shot him in the back of his head and escaped with the other stranger, taking back her jewels which the khan had kept as dowry. She must have been several months pregnant. I think that's what Rose was trying to tell me. Anyway, she decided this khan was her real father, so she hitched herself onto the clan as a kind of honorary aunt."

"She'd have been quite welcome if she was getting a regular allowance from England."

"She used it for dowries and things. What do you think?"

"I suppose it hangs together. What about what you call the real adventure? If Rose reported Fred correctly, this khan was not the only person Mrs Walsh had wiped out."

"Yes. When I saw her in her flat that time she told me about her mother's death. She sounded really bitter about it. Left in the snow with the spittle freezing on her cheek, like a foundered horse, she said. And she said it was how they were treated. I don't think she was making that up."

"Left by the khan?"

"I hadn't thought of that . . . No, I think she would have sounded different. She used to talk about the Tadzhiks in a much more detached way. I think she was talking about her real mother, who was one of the Belayevs' servants. You remember they used to make their servants act plays for them? I don't think it was Mrs Walsh's mother — she hinted it was her grandmother — who'd been the Grand Duke's mistress."

"You are introducing a new element."

"Not really. Didn't I tell you? Alex and Mr Brown were talking about it that evening. It started with Mrs Walsh looking like Granny, and whether she could be a Romanov too. There was a Grand Duke Aleksei. Mr Brown said he liked fast women and slow ships, and Alex said he preferred actresses to countesses. I think he must have given the grandmother the egg. That's why Mrs Walsh never sold it with the other jewels. It really was hers. She sold the ones she'd stolen from the Belayevs."

"You are going to tell me she killed them for the jewels."

"I expect some of them just died. It must have been a frightful journey. But, well, Fred did say she'd shot 'the others'. That means more than just the khan. It was sort of in the air those days, wasn't it — stories about servants rising up and massacring their masters? And I've sometimes wondered what they ate during the journey. Fred was terrified of her."

"You've met her, I haven't. You really think she was up to all that?"

"Oh, yes. Easily. That's what I meant about her being different from Maria. She didn't care about anybody else at all. She tried to make people nothing."

"What does that mean?"

"Well, I know you think we aren't really there at all. We're just a sort of compromise, but . . . ."

"That's a caricature of my position. The I that I think of as I is not an entity. It is an abstraction, a balance of opposing forces, but as such it is as real as, say, the British Constitution. Nobody can say precisely what the British Constitution is, or where it lies, but it is absurd to deny its existence."

"All right, let's call it a balance. What I was trying to say is you aren't allowed to go poking around interfering with other people's balances. Making them what you want them to be instead of what they are."

"Everybody does it."

"Almost everybody. It's what the GBP and the hacks are doing all the time to us. It's what I was trying to do to Janine, I suppose. It's what the terrorists keep trying to do not just to one or two people but to whole countries. It's what you tried to stop us doing to you when we got married. It's why Soppy went off her rocker . . . ."

"A factor, at most. There must have been an hereditary element, not to mention her relations with her mother."

"But it's still there. It's part of it. If it hadn't been for that she might've kept her balance. But what I'm trying to tell you is that Mrs Walsh didn't just go poking around, didn't just try and make people something else, she tried to make them nothing. What she did to Rose was the worst, but there was Fred, too. And Aunt Bea, I suppose, only actually you can't do that to Aunt Bea. She stays herself, in spite of anything you try."

"With most people the balance is extraordinarily resilient to change. The forces re-group, and a fresh balance, externally almost identical with the old one, is achieved."

"I hope so."

"A thought strikes me. The most extreme form of interference, obviously, is killing somebody. But isn't it almost as extreme to bring them into being in the first place?"

"Nonsense."

"In what way nonsense?"

"I'm too tired to think about it. I'll tell you tomorrow. Let's call it a day. Have you had enough concrete whatsits?"

"Particularities? I think so. Sleep well."

"Sleep well."

They kissed. Louise turned on her side and massaged the small of her back into the hollow above his hip. His arm was still stretched out beneath her neck. He would sleep on his back all night, mysteriously managing not to snore. She felt for his hand and held it. It was good of him to have let her talk her day through — he hadn't really wanted to — he'd much rather have stayed in his maze, but instead he'd actually listened, helped, paid attention to nuances . . . Like Soppy, she was tired of skeletons, and though these ones had mainly been of no real concern of hers she felt that at last she had taken them out of their shadowy cupboards and laid them in the earth where they belonged. They could all sleep now.

Piers was asleep already. Davy? England was four hours behind Baku, so it would be getting on for half past ten at Quercy. Helen might be in the nursery this very moment, doing a last check-up. If Davy was starting a cold she'd be in for a restless night. In Louise's mind the nursery lost scale. The cot and the bending figure dwindled, remote figures in a vast dim room. Needs another cot, needs populating, she thought. Drowsily she counted months. Joan had been keeping a six-week gap in the diaries, a clearing among the prisoning thickets of entries, a glade into which, if she got it right, Louise could drop her fawn. It was still a month too early to start. On the other hand she'd got it wrong with Davy, been a tiresome three weeks late . . . A girl this time please . . . You weren't supposed to say that, not even to think it . . . Louise remembered talking to Soppy about this sort of thing, just after the Garden Party. I was a bit too tough with her, she thought — hope she took no notice . . . Anyway, it's nonsense what Piers was saying, about it being interfering with someone else getting them born in the first place — it's just as interfering deciding not to. Remember to tell him in the morning.

Gently she ran her fingertips over the coarse-boned wrist and along the muscle towards the elbow.

After we've done the practical, she thought. Before he's started thinking. And the hell with the diaries.